I0769553

Sweet Obsession

HONEYSUCKLE TEXAS ★ BOOK 5

CHRIS KENISTON

Indie House Publishing

Indie House Publishing

MORE BOOKS
By Chris Keniston

Honeysuckle Texas
Sweet Beginnings
Sweet Surprise
Sweet Temptation
Sweet Deal
Sweet Obsession
Sweet Tomorrows
Sweet Redemption

The Billionaire Barons of Texas
Just One Date
Just One Spark
Just One Dance
Just One Take
Just One Taste
Just One Shot
Just One Chance
Just One Mistake
Just One Family
Just One Rodeo
Just One Surprise
Just One Look

Hart Land
Heather
Lily
Violet
Iris
Hyacinth
Rose
Calytrix
Zinnia

Poppy
Picture Perfect

Farraday Country
Adam
Brooks
Connor
Declan
Ethan
Finn
Grace
Hannah
Ian
Jamison
Keeping Eileen
Loving Chloe
Morgan
Neil
Owen
Paxton
Quinn

Honeymoon Series
Honeymoon for One
Honeymoon for Three
Honeymoon for Four
Honeymoon for Five
Honeymoon for Six
Honeymoon for Seven

Aloha Romance Series:
Aloha Texas
Almost Paradise
Mai Tai Marriage
Dive Into You
Look of Love
Love by Design
Love Walks In
Shell Game
Flirting with Paradise

Surf's Up Flirts:
(Aloha Series Companions)
Shall We Dance
Love on Tap
Head Over Heels
Perfect Match
Just One Kiss
It Had to Be You
Cat's Meow

CHAPTER ONE

"**H**eads up!"

Jillian sprang back just as a hammer sailed through the air, landing a few inches in front of her.

"Sorry about that." Garret slid down a support post with the ease of a fireman gliding down a steel pole on his way to save lives. "I missed the loop in my belt. You okay?"

Nodding, she smiled at her brother. This wouldn't be the first or last time since the new construction project began that she'd been bumped, dinged, or suffered a near miss. She had the black and blues to prove it. "No harm, no foul."

Lips pressed tightly together, Garret nodded, and falling into place beside his sister, scanned the finally complete frame of what would soon be the Sweet Ranch's new calving barn. The foundation had been poured weeks ago, and now the wooden bones stretched skyward, outlining the structure that for so many years had lived only in their father's notes and dreams. "Dad would love it."

All the siblings who'd worked today gathered in a line and nodded their agreement.

Propped against a stack of lumber, music drifted from Preston's phone—a smooth blend of easy listening rock and country that made the assembly feel a little less like work and a little more like a party.

Alice, their mother, gazed across the burgeoning structure, a soft, approving smile on her face. Mindlessly, her hand reached down to stroke the thick fur of her eldest son's dog, always faithfully at her side. "Charlie would be so proud."

"He really would." Garret eyed the scribbled notepaper tacked to a center post. Their father had mapped out a plan and everyone felt a surge of pride at reaching another milestone on the long to-do list. "We've managed to get most of the pastures improved the way he wanted—organic fertilization, got a handle on the worst of the weeds, and Preston's rotational grazing system seems to be working wonders."

"And that new baler Jim bought has been a godsend." Carson hammered a stray nail flush. "We finally managed to acquire a few more head of cattle last month. Not as many as we'd hoped for initially, but it's a start. Should help with the income stream a bit."

Consulting his tablet where he'd been tracking their progress, Preston nodded. "If we can get this barn finished before calving season starts, we'll be in good shape. Thank God for Carson's construction connections—saved us a fortune on the foundation and framing."

Alice walked over to a plywood storage closet they'd built into one corner of the frame—a necessary precaution after the mysterious disappearance of the stolen hay baler they'd found hidden in the line shack. She carefully placed a set of new power tools inside. "Speaking of mysteries, any more news on Ray or those other hands?"

Preston shook his head. "Nothing solid."

A timer chimed from Alice's phone. "Oh, that's my roast. You all keep working—dinner in an hour." She hurried toward the house.

The moment their mom was out of earshot, Jillian spun around to face her brother. "So what aren't you telling us?"

Rubbing the back of his neck, Preston sighed. "Sean Farraday called earlier today. Told me he'd bumped into Ray—or someone who looked exactly like him—working for the Brady ranch near them."

"Mr. Farraday found Ray? Does the sheriff have him?" A million things swirled through Jillian's mind, the first being how she'd love to be back in the old west when they happily drew and quartered cattle rustlers. Or maybe it was just tarred and feathered. Either would do.

"'Fraid not. Sean didn't say anything, played it casual. The guy claimed his name was John Smith. By the time Sean got a hold of Declan, Ray and all his gear was gone."

"For a stellar thief, not a very original alias." Rachel rolled her eyes and shook her head.

"Wait." Carson's head snapped around. "Why was Ray working? That doesn't make sense at all."

"Good point." Rachel joined them from where she'd been sorting lumber. "Considering how much money he must have squirreled away from everything he stole from us, why would he need to work at all? He should be on a beach in some country where he can't be extradited."

"If he's as smart as we thought, agreed." Preston shrugged again.

"Or he's lying low, trying to blend in," Garret suggested darkly.

"I'd like to stick with he's an idiot." Rachel flashed a fake smile. "Gives me hope we'll actually catch the S.O.B."

The conversation turned to their own finances—how much progress they'd made, yet how far they still had to go. Jillian felt the familiar weight of expectation settling on her shoulders. Four siblings down, four successful marriages that had brought crucial trust fund payments. Now it was her turn.

Just then, the music from Carson's phone shifted. The twangy country faded, replaced by the soft, intricate finger picking of an acoustic guitar, a melody that was both melancholic and hopeful. A familiar male voice, rich and unexpectedly gentle, began to sing—one of Blake Kirby's older, lesser-known tracks, from before the stadium tours and the chart-topping cross over anthems.

Garret paused. "That's a new one on Carson's playlist. I preferred his earlier songs to his country-rock hits."

Looking up, Rachel stopped to listen. "Hard to believe that we knew Blake when he was nothing more than one of Kade's buddies. Who knew all that fiddling with the guitar would take him to the top of the charts?"

Now Garret stepped away from the storage closet, shaking his head. "Funny, isn't it? Buys that bazillion-dollar place down near the Austin music scene, supposedly to be closer to family, and yet he hasn't set foot back in Honeysuckle in years."

"Why should he come home?" Preston reached for his hat. "He flies his family anywhere they want to see him on tour. From what I hear, his grandmother used to follow him around the country like a groupie."

That made Jillian chuckle. Sara Kirby was as feisty as they come. The old woman would probably outlive them all and still be dancing after everyone was gone.

Carson heaved a sigh. "Can't blame him. It's certainly easier than dealing with grapevine queen Iris Hathaway."

Her brothers were right. This town held very little for Blake Kirby. Only half-listening to the ongoing conversation, the music pulled Jillian back to a memory from years ago. She was a little girl again, sitting off to the side on the back porch. Kade and his friends, Blake among them, playing a game of touch football on the sprawling back lawn. An idea had struck Blake, mid-play. He'd grabbed his battered guitar from the back of his pickup, settled onto the porch steps, and oblivious to the shouts and laughter around him, began to coax a new tune from the strings. Jillian had sat, mesmerized, as scattered notes bloomed into that unforgettable, haunting melody now playing from Carson's phone. When he'd finally looked up, his fingers stilling on the frets, and seen her sitting there, listening so intently, he'd smiled. She'd never forgotten that smile, the raw beauty of the tune, or the boy who'd become a rock star.

The song ended, and the usual country twang returned, snapping Jillian back to the present, the ranch, their dilemma, and the sound of a ticking clock in her head reminding her that her time to find a partner in crime was running out.

A galaxy of phone screens held aloft, the audience swayed

dutifully as Blake Kirby played the last, fading note of the encore, "Honeysuckle Memories." With bittersweet lyrics about dusty roads and firefly nights, no one in this sprawling arena would likely understand the true origins. The applause washed over him, a familiar wave, warm and thunderous. The final show of this tour, tonight the crowd had been electric—singing every word back to him.

He offered a practiced bow, called out a "Thank you, goodnight!" into the mic that would be broadcast onto the massive screens, and strode off stage right. The roar of the crowd, the chants of "Kirby! Kirby!" were already beginning to recede as he navigated the labyrinth of backstage corridors, the sudden shift to organized chaos a well-rehearsed dance.

This was it. The West Coast was the end of the line for the USA "Wildfire" tour. Twelve months, numerous cities, and too many hotel rooms to count. He could already hear the pop of champagne corks from the band's dressing room down the hall; half of them were probably already making plans to celebrate with the usual entourage of hopefuls, industry hangers-on, and women whose names they wouldn't remember by morning.

He bypassed it all with a curt nod to Phil, his perpetually harried tour manager, who was already barking into two phones at once, and a brief wave to Milo. Compact and surprisingly unassuming for a man who could probably disable three assailants before they hit the floor, his bodyguard fell into step a few paces behind, a silent, ever-present shadow.

The transition from stage god, commanding the attention of tens of thousands, to solitary man in a sterile black SUV was always jarring, the familiar post-show restlessness settling in. In the presidential suite of the five-star hotel, the silence shrouded him like a heavy blanket, broken only by the distant hum of city traffic twenty floors below. Ignoring the artfully arranged platter of gourmet snacks and the chilled champagne waiting on the coffee table, he walked to the panoramic window. The city lights spread out below him like a carpet of fallen stars, beautiful but impersonal. He'd seen a thousand cities like it. After a while they all blurred into one.

He ran a hand through his already disheveled hair. Sleep was a distant rumor. The adrenaline that had carried him through two and a half hours of performance was still a live current under his skin, thrumming with restless energy. He picked up his oldest, most battered acoustic—the one that had seen him through countless late nights in dingy college bars and even earlier, quieter nights on his grandmother's porch back in Honeysuckle. Its scarred wood felt more familiar, more real, than any of the high-end, custom-made instruments that now populated his collection.

His fingers found the strings, not with the practiced precision of his stage show, but with a hesitant, searching touch. A new riff, something softer than his recent chart topping hits, began to form under his restless touch. It was a wisp of a melody, something that had come to him unbidden, the way tunes used to arrive before writing music became a job, a product to be packaged and sold. This felt different, purer. He played it again, the notes hanging in the quiet air, more honest than anything he'd put on the last album.

Blake lost track of time as he worked through the progression, adding flourishes, finding the heart of the song that wanted to emerge. This was what he'd fallen in love with—not the screaming crowds or sold-out stadiums, but these quiet moments when music created itself through his hands.

The shrill ring of his phone cut through the melody, jarring him back to the present. Two in the morning. Who on earth...? He glanced at the caller ID, a frown creasing his brow. His grandmother. Sara Kirby. A wave of affection, quickly followed by a prickle of unease, washed over him. Grams never called this late. Or for some, this early.

He swiped to answer, the new melody dissolving. "Grams?"

"Blake, darling!" Her voice, usually a warm, Texas drawl, sounded unusually bright, almost unnervingly chipper for what was nearly four in the morning Texas time.

"Is something wrong?"

"Of course not. I bet you thought I forgot, didn't you?"

"Forgot?"

"Your birthday."

Setting the guitar against the wall, Blake leaned back into the stiff hotel chair. "Birthday?" Maybe she was sleep calling; because he and she both knew his birthday was months away.

"A grandmother never forgets her favorite grandson's special day." He could hear the smile in her voice.

"Grams, I'm your *only* grandson."

"Pfft. That's semantics. You're still my favorite."

Despite his mounting confusion over this odd hour phone call, Blake found himself smiling. "You got me there, but why are you up at four in the morning?"

"Morning? It's the middle of the afternoon." Her tone shifted to one of admonishing adult. "I just had a cup of tea and wanted to call you before you thought I'd forgotten your special day."

They talked for a little longer, Grams chatting about neighbors and weather and asking about friends from high school he hadn't seen in close to a decade. When she finally said goodbye, claiming she needed to start dinner, he was left staring at his phone. What the heck was going on?

CHAPTER TWO

The lunchtime lull had settled over Heaven Scent, leaving Jillian with a rare quiet moment. Her mind still churning over the morning's conversation with her brothers, the familiar weight of the ranch's precarious finances, a burden she shared with all her siblings, pressed down even amidst the fragrant chaos of her candle shop. She needed to move, get some fresh air. A walk, a chance to clear her head before tackling the displays for her latest batch of Honeysuckle candles.

"Carol," Jillian grabbed a protein bar from the desk drawer and waved at her part-time employee, "I'm going to have lunch al fresco today."

Her words made Carol chuckle softly. The woman was the best employee Jillian had ever had. "Take your time."

With another wave and a smile, Jillian was out the door and strolling down Main Street. Honeysuckle was in its usual weekday rhythm –familiar faces nodding greetings, tourists happily laden with packages from their souvenir purchases or joining the locals in a casual game of corn hole at the park. Despite the feel of the warm Texas sun on her face and the joyful smiles of everyone she encountered, the weight of the ranch situation sat heavily on her shoulders. Four siblings married, four trust fund payments secured, and now it was her turn to contribute to the plan to save the ranch. Something she would gladly do, except she'd had zero success so far finding a husband willing to enter into a business only marriage, especially one with the Sweet family's particular requirements.

Taking a seat at the edge of the park, she hoped watching the children playing gleefully on the swings would help ease the growing anxiety that gnawed at her stomach. Peeling the wrapper away from her lunch, she let the warmth of the day and the sound of laughter, both from the children in the park and the group of older men across the way engaged in a lively game of corn hole, strip away some of the stress.

For a long moment, it seemed to be working. Her gaze wandered up Elm Street. This older section of Honeysuckle was one of her favorites. The side streets held charming houses ranging from cozy craftsman bungalows to larger Victorian homes. Elm Street was her favorite. A burst of colorful flowers decorated every home. She especially liked the fuchsia blooms from Mrs. Kirby's Chinese fringe flowers. Mrs. Carrington had wonderful arrays of cornflowers and black-eyed susans, but even Mrs. Dorman's clusters of hydrangeas couldn't compete with Mrs. Kirby's green thumb.

About to return her attention to the old men cheering like a couple of kids at a Friday night football game, a lone figure making its way up the street caught her eye. Not that anyone walking up Elm Street would be unusual, but this man was not typical. His hands in his pockets, head hanging low, and wearing a fully extended dark hoodie—in this heat? The guy stood out like a cowboy in Manhattan. Hunched the way he was, he seemed to be trying to fold into himself, hide from the world.

Everyone was entitled to a need for privacy or a little solitude, unless the reason he was skulking about from house to house in the shadows of the street was because he was up to no good.

Pushing to her feet, Jillian moved casually toward the curb, her gaze remaining fixed on the figure now turning off the sidewalk and crossing the line of flowers in Mrs. Kirby's front yard. Every instinct she had told her this was a crime waiting to happen. Pulling her phone out of from her pocket, she inched her way up Elm Street. Keeping her back to the wall of the old pharmacy, she dialed the sheriff's office. One ring, two rings. At the end of the brick building, she had a clear view of the man fiddling with the windows on the front porch of Mrs. Kirby's house. A break-in. In broad daylight. In Honeysuckle.

"Honeysuckle police," Madge's voice came over the phone loud a clear. A little too loud.

Lowering her voice, Jillian quickly explained she was tracking a burglar on Elm Street.

"There's probably a good reason, but just in case, you stay put and out of sight. I'll dispatch the sheriff," Madge said.

Before Jillian could agree or disagree, the call was disconnected. All she could think was what if Mrs. Kirby was inside? Alone? Defenseless? Jillian glanced over her shoulder—no sign of the sheriff. Redirecting her gaze up the street, the character in the hoodie had gone up the side yard and disappeared from sight. Not a good sign.

It took her all of five seconds to decide, sheriff or no sheriff, she could not let anything happen to sweet Sara Kirby. That old woman was a staple of good cheer around town. Jillian still could not stand by and do nothing. Clutching her purse in front of her, she moved at a slightly faster clip up the street and thanked heaven the intruder hadn't shut the front gate. The last thing she wanted was for the dumb thing to creak and announce her arrival.

Scurrying across the short front yard, she leaned into one of those beautiful shrubs she so admired and peered around the corner. Son of a ... two sneaker clad feet attached to a pair of dark jeans, dangled from a side window. Definitely up to no good.

Blake muttered a curse under his breath, his fingers fumbling with the stubborn window latch. He should be on a private jet to Fiji right now, decompressing from the tour, not trying to break into his own grandmother's house like a second-rate cat burglar. He ran the conversation with his mother through his mind for the tenth time. "Grams is fine, Blake, just a little more forgetful these days."

Forgetful was one thing. Wishing him a happy birthday months early and thinking it was afternoon at four in the morning was something else entirely. He'd seen the subtle decline in one of his bandmate's parents, the early stages of dementia that everyone tried to dismiss as simple old age. He had to see for himself, know for himself. He couldn't shake the image of his feisty, independent grandmother alone and confused.

He'd driven straight through from the Dallas airport, his nerves shot, his patience frayed. He'd parked a few blocks away. In an effort to avoid being recognized, he'd decided a dark hoodie was the best option for slipping in and out of town unnoticed. The problem: he'd forgotten how merciless the hot Texas sun could be. In the heat, the dang hoodie had become his own personal sauna. Sweat had trickled down his back like the mighty Mississippi, but he couldn't risk taking it off. Not in Honeysuckle. The moment someone recognized him, Iris Hathaway would have the gossip spread from here to Austin before he could blink.

With every step, he'd scanned the quiet streets. Even his mother didn't have a clue he was here. Didn't know he'd canceled three meetings to make this trip. If his mom was right and his grandmother was merely momentarily forgetful, then he'd slip out of town the same way he came in. No fuss, no fans, no explanations. But deep down, he didn't believe that or he wouldn't be suffering through this cloak-and-dagger effort in the sweltering heat to check for himself.

But first, he had to find her. The problem: where the heck was the old woman? Her car wasn't in the driveway, and she wasn't answering her phone. He couldn't exactly wander around Main Street waiting for her to come home. Not without being spotted.

The charming houses of Elm Street with their vibrant flower gardens would normally have brought back fond memories, but today they just made his mission more complicated. Too many nosy neighbors. Too many windows. Too many eyes that might recognize the prodigal son of Honeysuckle, even with his face hidden.

He approached his grandmother's house from the side, staying close to the flowering shrubs that had always been her pride and joy. The fuchsia blooms of her Chinese fringe flowers were as bright as ever. At least that hadn't changed.

Blake tried the front door first—locked. Then the back—also locked. Good for her, but inconvenient for him. He moved methodically around the house, checking each window, giving them gentle pushes.

"Come on, Grams," he whispered. His fingers found the sill of the side window, hidden behind an enormous hydrangea bush. He pushed upward, and to his relief, it slid open with a soft creak.

"Aha! Finally." A smile crept across his face. "Really need to talk to her about home security, though."

He hoisted himself up, grabbing the windowsill and pushing the screen in carefully. The movement caused his hood to fall back slightly, and he quickly tugged it forward again. He'd come this far without being recognized; he wasn't about to blow it now.

Getting through the window was more challenging than he remembered from his teenage years. His legs dangled awkwardly as he worked to get his upper body through the opening. The smell of his grandmother's house—lemon polish and cinnamon—brought a wave of nostalgia so strong it almost made him pause midway. Lifting his gaze, he scanned the familiar living room—doilies, photos of him at every awkward stage of life. This had once been his safe place. Before the fame, before the crowds, before the constant scrutiny. When he was just Blake, the kid who played guitar on the porch while his grandmother Sara hummed along and shelled peas.

Stomach balancing precariously, sucking in a fortifying breath, he gripped the sill and swung one leg over. Halfway in, still bent awkwardly at the waist, the unwanted sound of footsteps approaching from outside sent him scurrying the rest of the way into the house, landing with a soft thud on the hardwood floor.

Somehow, he knew it was not his grandmother. His suspicions confirmed when a soft but determined voice, a decidedly sharp and feminine voice, sliced through the quiet.

"Stop right there or I'll shoot!"

CHAPTER THREE

"**J**illian Sweet, what in the Sam Hill do you think you're doing?"

The familiar, exasperated tone of Sheriff Brody cut through the tense air. She knew how to handle a gun, and knew she had the upper hand on the intruder, but still, it was nice to have some back-up. Despite how her heart hammered a frantic beat against her ribs, her gaze never wavered from the hooded figure now frozen on the hardwood floors of Mrs. Kirby's living room, and her hands, gripping the 9mm Smith and Wesson she kept in her purse, remained calm and steady. Charlie Sweet would be proud of his daughter. Both she and her sister had learned how to shoot a gun when they were about nine years old. By the time they were both in high school, there was little doubt anyone would ever get the upper hand on a Sweet as long as they were packing. And they were always packing.

"Didn't Madge on dispatch tell you to wait for me?" The sheriff's heavy boot steps crunched on the gravel of the side path before he appeared beside her, his substantial frame a sudden, grounding presence. He didn't yell; he just sighed, the sound of a man who'd seen this kind of stubbornness from a Sweet before. He gently touched the top of her extended hand, his fingers applying firm, yet gentle pressure to point the barrel of the gun toward the neatly trimmed lawn. "I know you know how to use that thing, but the last thing I need is for you to shoot someone's foot off."

"Not where I'm aiming."

"Yeah, that's what I'm afraid of. Generally, I prefer my B&E suspects alive and able to answer a few questions."

"As long as I can say the same for Mrs. Kirby." The sincere concern made Jillian's voice sound tight. Images of the sweet, feisty old woman harmed by this skulking intruder prodded at her gut like a hot poker. "He was breaking in, Sheriff. In broad daylight. What was I supposed to do, offer him a glass of sweet tea?"

"I see that." The sheriff shifted his focus past her, his own voice hardening into the official tone he used when things got serious. "Alright, son. Hands where I can see 'em. Stand up straight and turn around. Slowly."

The figure complied, unfolding himself from the hardwood surface, rising to his full height, he raised his hands in surrender. As the suspect turned, Sheriff Brody took a step forward, reached through the window, and with one quick tug, pulled the hoodie away from the man's face.

Jillian's world stuttered to a halt. The gun in her hand suddenly felt impossibly heavy. Mussed sandy blond hair, a strong jawline, shadowed with stubble, and those eyes— startlingly green eyes she hadn't seen in person since she was a kid, now wide with a mixture of apprehension and weary resignation could only be one person—Blake Kirby.

"Lord love a duck." The sheriff's stern expression melted into one of pure, dumbfounded disbelief. He stared for a long moment, a frown creasing his brow as he processed the impossible. "Boy, what in the name of all that's holy are you doing breaking into your own grandmother's house?"

Yep. Blake Kirby. The rock star. The boy from her youth whose memory was tangled up with the scent of summer nights and the sound of a guitar. Before he could answer, another voice, chipper and utterly familiar, floated from the front walkway.

"Sheriff Brody, what's all this commotion?"

The sheriff and Jillian both took a step back, making way for the homeowner now heading up the path with a bag of groceries in one arm and her handbag in the other. Jillian's gaze dropped to the gun in her hand and quickly secured the safety, then hurriedly stored the gun in the locked compartment of her handbag.

Coming to a sudden stop, Sara Kirby placed a hand on her hip, and fixed the sheriff with a withering glare that could have curdled milk. "And what exactly, Martin Brody, do you think you are you doing to my favorite grandson?"

Blake dropped his hands, a look of profound, soul-deep relief washing over his handsome face. "Grams! I was so worried. I called, you didn't answer... I thought something was wrong."

"Pish posh. I was at the market getting ingredients for your favorite pie." She beamed at Blake, a vision of grandmotherly adoration, then her sharp eyes narrowed, landing first on Jillian, then at the purse where she'd stowed her handgun. "And you, young lady. Jillian Sweet. Threatening my grandson with that firearm? Has the world gone completely mad?"

Jillian felt a hot, mortifying blush creep up her neck "I... I thought he was a burglar, Mrs. Kirby. He was climbing in the window. I'm so, so sorry."

"Well, you've got good intentions and a steady hand, I'll give you that." Mrs. Kirby flashed a familiar smile before turning her full attention back to the sheriff. "Now, is it now illegal for a boy to visit his grandmother?"

"No, ma'am." Sheriff Brody sighed, tipping his hat toward Mrs. Kirby, a gesture of respect and surrender. "I'm assuming you won't be pressing charges?"

Now Jillian understood why the cliché *if looks could kill* remained popular in modern culture. The aging woman gave the sheriff a look so potent, so full of unspoken history and small-town authority, it made both Jillian and Blake chuckle under their breath. The sheriff held up his hands and began backing away toward the street, shaking his head. "Thought so," he mumbled, turning away. "You all have a nice day now. And next time, son, try the door."

Not till Sheriff Brody was completely out of sight did Blake's pulse finally slow to a normal rhythm.

"Well." His grandmother turned and sporting an even brighter smile than moments before, faced the woman who only moments ago had been pointing a loaded gun at him. "No point in standing out here growing roots. I baked a pie this morning. Come on in and I'll cut us a slice."

Jillian didn't get a chance to do more than sputter like a clogged engine. It was obvious to anyone within ear shot that his grandmother wasn't expecting an argument. Heaving a loud sigh, the girl he hadn't seen in what felt like forever waved her hands and hurried after his grandmother. "Mrs. Kirby, I'm so sorry about the misunderstanding—" her voice carried through the open window.

"Don't you worry yourself. Any good neighbor would have done the same. The important thing is you didn't shoot him."

The front door swung open in time for Blake to see Jillian. Moving quickly, he took the grocery bag from his grandmother as she stepped inside. "Let me get those for you, Grams."

"Thank you, dear." She patted his cheek, the familiar gesture tightening his throat. "Put those in the kitchen. And for heaven's sake, take off that ridiculous hoodie. You look like you're planning to rob a bank."

He ducked into the kitchen, grateful for something to do. The layout was as familiar as his own heartbeat—glasses by the sink, plates to the left, silverware in the drawer below. Grams was a creature of habit, which made that disoriented phone call all the more disturbing.

On his heels, his grandmother opened a cabinet by the sink, pulling out a stack of plates. "Set these down on the coffee table in the living room."

"Yes, ma'am."

"Come back for the tea."

He nodded again. Unable just yet to meet Jillian's gaze, he set the dishes on the antique table and muttered, "Be right back."

On the counter, his grandmother had set a pitcher, silverware, napkins and glasses on a tray. "Take this and I'll bring the pie."

Setting the tray down beside the plates, he couldn't help but think how normal everything seemed. Nothing about his grandmother's behavior seemed odd or out of place. Not a single word had set off any alarm bells. So why did he still feel more uneasy than a cat in a room full of rocking chairs?

Quietly perched on the edge of the Queen Anne wingback, Jillian looked like she might bolt any second. Blake sank into the sofa, the cushions sighing under his weight. The air in the room still, his grandmother taking her time slicing the fresh pie, he finally looked at Jillian, really looked at her. The years had been kind. More than kind. The fiery kid he remembered was still there in her green eyes, but now there was a poised, capable woman staring back at him. A woman who, he reminded himself, had been perfectly willing to shoot him a few minutes ago.

"So." Sliding a slice of pie onto a dish and holding it out for her guest, Grams smiled sweetly. Too sweetly. "Tell me what's so important it had you flying all the way from California and climbing through my window like a teenager sneaking into a house before his parents have had time to figure out he'd been out all night."

"It started the other night when you called to wish me a happy birthday."

Her brow furrowed. "Your birthday? But your birthday isn't for months. Why would I do that?"

Her response was so clear, so lucid, that for a second, Blake questioned his own memory. Had he dreamed the call? Had the exhaustion of the tour finally made him crack? But he knew he hadn't. He remembered every bewildering word.

He leaned forward. "You called at four in the morning, wished me happy birthday then told me you had to get off the phone to cook dinner."

"Cook dinner at four in the morning?" Brows arched high quickly buckled over her narrowed gaze. "I don't suppose you were... drinking when you got this phone call?"

His days of drinking and partying from tour to tour were long gone. "No," he shook his head, "but the call did worry me."

"Did you have sushi? That raw fish probably gives lots of people nightmares. I mean, really, why would anyone want to eat raw fish?"

This all sounded so much like the grandmother he'd known all his life and loved dearly. But he knew he wasn't dreaming when she called. Had he been asleep, maybe he would have believed he'd imagined the whole thing, but he'd been wide awake. Now he was more confused than ever.

"Oh, my. I forgot the ice cream." Grams sprang up from her seat. "I'll be right back."

As his grandmother's back disappeared into the kitchen, Jillian cleared her throat. "I really am sorry about before, with the gun."

Tearing his gaze away from the kitchen doorway, he leveled his gaze with hers. "While I prefer not to have loaded guns pointed at me, it's good to know folks are watching out for Grams."

"Always." Jillian's smile was sweet, soft and at the same time, radiant. "We all love Mrs. Kirby."

His attention darted back to the kitchen where he could hear his grandmother puttering about, no doubt scooping ice cream into bowls.

"You're really worried?" Jillian's voice came out low and laced with concern.

"Yeah." He blew out a heavy sigh. "I didn't dream that call. She was totally confused."

"She seems fine now."

"I know. Which has *me* totally confused." He shook his head. "I can't leave. For all I know, that call could have been caused by a stroke, or…worse."

Jillian's brows buckled. "Worse?"

"The call reminded me of a friend's mom right before she was diagnosed with dementia."

A small gasp escaped from Jillian's throat as her gaze drifted to the kitchen where his grandmother was now closing the freezer door.

"She seems fine now."

He nodded. She did. But he couldn't get that call out of his head. "I can't leave now and pretend nothing happened. But I can't stay in town either." He raked a hand through his hair. "It would be a circus."

Jillian's eyes were thoughtful. "What about the Sweet Ranch?"

"What about it?"

"You could stay with us. We're far enough out of town that you could stay out of the limelight, but close enough that you can check on your grandmother and visit your parents. At least while you figure out what to do about your grandmother."

Growing up, the Sweet Ranch had been like a second home to him, but that was back before he and Kade had left Honeysuckle to follow their dreams. Could he take her up on it? Did he have any other choice? Something was definitely not right with Grams, and until he figured out what, he wasn't going anywhere. He sure hoped the old adage was true and there really was no place like home.

CHAPTER FOUR

Jillian scraped the last bit of ice cream from her bowl, the sweet apple and cinnamon lingering on her tongue. Mrs. Kirby's pies were legendary in Honeysuckle, and this one lived up to the reputation. Across from her, Blake watched his grandmother with an intensity that reminded her of a hawk tracking its prey—alert, focused, and missing nothing.

"Blake, dear, you've hardly touched your pie." Mrs. Kirby gestured to his barely eaten slice. "Don't tell me you've gone Hollywood on me with some fancy diet."

"No, ma'am." Blake smiled, though Jillian noticed it didn't quite reach his eyes. "Just enjoying the conversation."

Pushing to her feet, Mrs. Kirby collected her and Jillian's empty bowls and fixed her grandson with a look that was pure, unfiltered affection. "I'll clean up while you finish your pie. Then I'll head upstairs quick and straighten out your old room. Won't take me long to move a few things out of the way and get fresh linens."

Blake glanced at Jillian, a silent confirmation passing between them. "Actually, Grams, you don't have to go to any trouble for me. I'm going to stay at the Sweet Ranch."

A bowl in each hand, Mrs. Kirby blinked at her grandson. "The ranch? Well," a pensive glare shifted to a wide smile, "what a nice idea. You and Kade can catch up properly. It'll be just like old times. Just don't go getting into any mischief. You're grown men now." Sara Kirby turned on her heel and scurried into the kitchen.

Blake flinched, his own smile tightening at the edges. His grandmother had momentarily slipped, her timeline blurring the years. Kade hadn't been around to get into mischief with Blake for a very long time. It was a small slip, the kind anyone could make, but in this context, it felt like a crack appearing in a perfectly polished veneer, revealing the fragility beneath. His jaw slightly agape, Blake's gaze met hers. "I'm not imagining it."

Even though it wasn't really a question, she shook her head. "If Kade being in the military was a recent change, I might think it had slipped her mind, but he's been gone as long as you have."

"I know." His gaze on the kitchen door, he leaned back and sighed. "That's what's scaring me."

"I need to get back to the store before someone thinks I've been kidnapped by aliens. I assume you have a car?" Jillian asked.

He nodded. "Rented it at the airport. Parked it around the corner."

"All right. Let me get back to work, let Carol know I'm going home early, and I'll come back and get you. I don't think we want a repeat of you lurking through the streets like a common prowler." She hurried over to the kitchen doorway and leaned in. "Mrs. Kirby, thank you so much for the pie. It was delicious. But I should be getting back to my shop."

"Of course, dear. Don't be a stranger." Sara Kirby left the dishes on the counter and turned to wrap Jillian in a surprisingly strong, lilac-scented hug. "And thank you for looking out for me, even if you were a little overzealous about it."

Sharp Mrs. Kirby was back front and center. If the situation weren't so alarming, Jillian might have found the shift funny.

She left Blake on the porch, turning back once to see him leaning against the railing, looking for all the world like the boy she used to know, just with broader shoulders and a heavier weight on them.

Jillian hurried down the street toward Heaven Scent, her mind racing faster than her feet. Holy cow. Was she really about to drive Blake Kirby to his car and then lead him back to her family's ranch? Was this really happening? Blake Kirby, the boy from her youth, the rock star from her daydreams, was going to be staying at her house. The whole situation felt insanely surreal. Shoving open the door to Heaven Scent, she momentarily wondered if this wasn't all a dream. Any second now, her alarm would go off and she'd awaken to the realization that chores needed to be done and Blake Kirby was somewhere else in the world making music that made women swoon.

Pulling her car up a few minutes later, seeing none other than the one and only Blake Kirby standing in the doorway of his grandmother's house told her if this was a dream—it was a lulu.

Spotting her at the curb, he popped his head inside, hugged his grandmother, hurried down the front steps and jumped into her car with the speed and tension of a man who had just robbed a bank.

"If I were you, I wouldn't quit your day job." She pulled away from the curb but saw his brows buckle in confusion before an honest grin took over his face and low rumble of laughter escaped his chest.

"I guess I would make an awful cat burglar."

"The worst." Jillian smiled. "I mean, who wears a hoodie in ninety-degree heat? You might as well have worn a sign that said, 'Suspicious Character.'"

His laugh was deeper this time, his shoulders relaxing slightly as he pointed down the street. "Black SUV is mine."

Her brow lifted and she shook her head. "Really? You couldn't find something a little more conspicuous?"

Looking meek, the man smiled and shrugged. "They didn't have any pick-up trucks available."

At least he still remembered what most people drove in this part of the state. Pulling up beside the vehicle, she watched him slip from her car into his, then waited for him to pull out behind her before she stepped on the gas. If this wasn't a dream, life was about to get very, very interesting.

Blake's rental bounced over the cattle guard, the metallic rumble sending a rush of nostalgia through him. Following Jillian Sweet's car up the long gravel drive felt like coming home. The sprawling ranch house came into view, just as he remembered—a welcoming fortress of stone and timber against the vast Texas terrain. He cut the engine of the SUV, the silence that followed amplifying the sudden thud of his own heart.

Jillian was already out of her car, waiting for him by the porch steps. She looked small against the backdrop of the massive house, but there was a steadiness in her stance, an easy confidence he didn't remember. Of course, the last time he'd really seen her, she'd been a scrawny kid with a talent for being underfoot whenever Kade had friends over. Before he could join her, the front door swung open and Alice Sweet bustled onto the porch, wiping her hands on her apron.

Her smile was as wide and warm as he remembered. "Blake Kirby? Is that really you?" Before he could say a word, she was off the front porch, standing in front of him, and pulling him into a tight bear hug.

Instantly, the stardom, the tour buses, the screaming crowds, all of it faded away. Now he was simply Blake Kirby, Kade's best friend, standing in the front yard of his second home.

"Took you long enough to remember where you belong." Alice Sweet took a half step in retreat, her eyes twinkling, her tone a perfect blend of sweet welcome and gentle scolding.

"Sorry, ma'am." He couldn't think of anything else to say, or meant anything more sincerely. He should have come back sooner. Shouldn't have hidden away.

"It is so good to see you, son. But you're too thin."

He laughed. A real, unforced sound. "It's good to see you too, Mrs. Sweet. And I promise, I'm eating."

Alice Sweet's gaze shifted to her daughter, then back to

him. Linking elbows with him, she began walking toward the house. "Let's go inside and then you can tell me what brings you here after all these years."

Jillian fell into step beside her mother. "Blake's here for his grandmother."

"Sara?" Mrs. Sweet's step halted. "Is something wrong?"

"I don't know." Blake pulled his arm from hers and opened the screen door.

"That's why he's here." As they walked to the kitchen, Jillian brought her mother up to date on Blake's concerns.

Taking a seat at the familiar kitchen table, the same one that had been here since he was a kid, he filled in the details for his best friend's mother.

"I'm so sorry, sweetie." Mrs. Sweet's expression softened instantly with motherly concern. "Jillian did the right thing. Of course, you'll stay here. We have plenty of room. But I wouldn't hold my breath on keeping you a secret for long." She held her hand up. "Don't get me wrong, we'll do our best, but eventually, someone is bound to recognize you coming and going from your grandmother's house."

He knew she was right, but he just couldn't deal with the small-town grapevine and any media bedlam that would follow once word got out that he was in town without stone walls and iron gates to keep him safe. "Which is why I thought I'd wait till after dark to go talk to Mom and Dad."

Alice shook her head. "You'd need more than the cover of night to hide from the grapevine. I'll call Betty and have them come here for dinner tonight."

It wasn't a question or even a suggestion. As sure as he knew his last album had topped the country rock charts, he knew that his parents would be sitting at the Sweet dining room table tonight.

"Supper's already started. I'll just head upstairs and get your room ready."

"I'll help." Jillian pushed to her feet.

"No." Alice shook her head. "This isn't a two-person job." She scurried out of the kitchen and up the stairs, leaving Blake and Jillian in the sudden quiet of the late afternoon.

"Your mom is one of a kind."

"She is." A soft smile touched Jillian's lips. She gestured toward the back of the house. "It'll be a bit before everyone straggles in from their day. I'll pour us a couple of drinks and we can sit out on the back porch."

A sudden memory of Alice Sweet's strawberry lemonade made his mouth water. "Lemonade?"

Jillian giggled, much like she did when she was only ten years old, but there was no doubt in his mind she was far from a little girl now. "Two strawberry lemonades coming up."

The drinks poured, each with a glass in hand, he followed her out the door to the sprawling back porch. He remembered this place. This was where the real heart of the Sweet family always seemed to beat. He sank onto one of the many rockers on the massive porch, the familiar creak of the wooden seats a sound straight from his youth.

Jillian took the seat beside him, pushing off gently with her feet. For a long moment, they were quiet; the only sound a distant lowing of cattle.

"I remember you and Rachel used to sit on those steps right there and watch us boys play football for hours."

She laughed, a light, musical sound. "From where we sat, you all just looked more like a chaotic pile of arms and legs rather than an organized game with rules and regulations." Turning her head, her gaze met his. "So, now what do you plan to do about your grandmother?"

The question brought the weight of the day rushing back. "I've spoken with a band member whose mother had dementia. She'll need some basic tests done first. I've got a list of the best neurologists in the county. I'd prefer to take her to UT Southwestern but I know better than to think she'd be willing to go all the way to Dallas if she doesn't think there's anything wrong with her."

She nodded, her expression full of an empathy that felt like a balm on a raw wound, when unexpectedly a hint of a smile teased at one corner of her mouth. "I don't suppose you've considered slipping her a mickey, because I don't think there will be any other way to get her to any doctor, never mind a specialist."

It shouldn't have been funny, and yet, it was. His grandmother's feistiness was one of the things that he'd always loved about that old woman. He had no idea what was going to happen next, but there was one thing he was most definitely sure of, coming here had been the right thing to do—and maybe slipping his grandmother a mickey wasn't such a bad idea either.

CHAPTER FIVE

Nursing the strawberry lemonade Jillian had poured for him, Blake sat in the rocker next to hers, his gaze fixed on the sprawling pastureland that melted into the distance. As if sensing her gaze, he turned his head, his lips momentarily pressed into a thin line. "I know it's too late," his voice came out low and raspy, as if he hadn't spoken for days, "but I'm so very sorry for your loss and that I couldn't make it back for your dad's funeral. I wanted to be here. Your dad meant a great deal to me."

The heartfelt sincerity in his voice tightened her throat. "We knew you were on tour. We got the flowers you sent. They were beautiful."

"It wasn't enough. He was always good to me." A faint, sad smile touched his lips. "And to all of Kade's knucklehead friends. He never once got mad, not even when we accidentally backed his new truck into the fence post and tore off the bumper."

"I'd forgotten about that." She bit back a laugh. "Dad loved that truck, but he loved you boys more."

The screen door squeaked open and slammed shut. "The place is so quiet; I didn't think anyone was home." Stretching his shoulders, Garret quickly scanned the length of the porch, his head jerking to a stop when his gaze fell on their guest. "Blake?"

A slow easy smile took over the musician's face. "The one and only."

Before Garrett could say another word, the gravel path crunched under arriving footsteps. From the barn, Carson made his way toward the house with their lone ranch hand Clint on his heels. As his younger brother had done, the second eldest brother came to a screeching halt the minute his gaze settled on their guest. "Holy…" Within seconds, he was up on the porch and pulling Blake into a back-slapping hug. "What the heck are you doing here?"

"Good to see you too." Blake chuckled. For the first time all afternoon, his smile reached his eyes and the twinkle did a funny thing to Jillian's insides.

"Nice to meet you." Clint tipped his head at Blake; if he knew who their guest was, their ranch hand didn't let on. "I'll go on inside and report to your mother."

A few words were exchanged between Carson and the foreman and the next thing she knew, Garret nudged Blake's shoulder with his own. "So, this is what a rock star on vacation looks like? A little less glitter than I expected."

Carson, a wry grin spreading across his face, joined in, leaning against the porch railing. "Don't let him fool you, Garret. He saves the glitter for the stage and, of course, all his groupies."

The teasing was a test, an invitation back into their world, and Jillian watched, fascinated, as Blake just shook his head, a genuine laugh rumbling in his chest, a decade of fame and distance easily melting away. "You guys haven't changed a bit. Still think playing a guitar isn't real work, huh?"

A tangle of lighthearted shoves and pokes ensued, her brothers continuing to pepper Blake with questions about life on the road, the women he must have on every continent, and just how great life must be without ever having to get up before dawn to mend a fence line in the freezing cold.

It was the timeless dance of male friendship—the teasing, the physical contact, the unspoken affection beneath the ribbing—a language they'd all spoken since they were boys shooting hoops in the driveway and dreaming of bigger things.

"I'm guessing no one is hungry tonight?" Her mom stood in the back doorway shaking her head. "Blake, your mom just texted that they'll be here in ten minutes."

Clint slid past their mother, tipping his hat at Jillian as

he walked back to his bunkhouse. Inside, her sisters-in-law were helping set the table, already chatting about the celebrity under their roof. A few more minutes and hugs and kisses and a few happy tears abounded as the Kirby's arrived, making Jillian think that maybe they hadn't seen their son in a pretty long time as well.

Conversation flowed easily over dinner. But Mr. and Mrs. Kirby didn't seem to think there was anything to be concerned about with Blake's grandmother.

"The woman is pushing ninety. She's bound to forget a thing or two," his dad insisted.

Clearly, as far as Blake's parents were concerned, the old woman's occasional memory lapses—and from the conversation, it sounded like they happened more often than Blake thought—was normal behavior for a woman her age. Now Jillian understood why Blake felt the need to come to Honeysuckle and see for himself. Concern was clearly etched on his face. He still smiled at his parents, nodded, and took in every word they said, but it was clear he didn't agree. And frankly, neither did she. Up until today, Sara Kirby always asked for Kade and how he was doing while deployed. Never had she forgotten he didn't live at the ranch anymore.

In the end, his parents agreed to help convince Mrs. Kirby to have some testing done and Blake promised to stay as long as was necessary to make sure his grandmother was in good health or getting the best care needed if she wasn't. He hugged his mother tightly at the door, promised to visit tomorrow, and then gave his dad a hug so tight she thought one of them might snap.

This was the Blake she remembered—thoughtful, kind. And yet, he was more. The genuine worry he held for his grandmother chipped away at the assumptions she'd built up over the years. She'd always figured he didn't come back to Honeysuckle because he'd outgrown it, that his rock-star life had made his small-town roots, and the people in them, feel unimportant. Now she was sure that she couldn't have been more wrong.

Without a word, Blake's mom had pulled him into another fierce hug, this one even tighter than the one she'd given him moments before. "It's so good to have you home," she mumbled against his shoulder. "So good."

Patting her back, equally overwhelmed with a rush of emotion, he tried not to squeeze her too hard. "I know Mom." The funny thing, he truly did. Nothing could have prepared him for how in only a few hours he could feel so very much at home.

Inside the sprawling living room, the family slowly decompressed from dinner and the day's work. Preston and Sarah Sue occupied the couch. Carson had claimed the leather chair, his son in his lap. Garret leaned against the mantel, his wife in the kitchen with Alice. Only Rachel and her new husband were absent, having retired early for the night. Of course, they were most newly of the newlyweds so no surprise there. The easy familiarity of it all wrapped around him like a warm blanket, a reminder of everything he'd missed through the years.

Just then, Alice walked in from the kitchen, wiping her hands on a dish towel. She looked utterly exhausted but satisfied. Her gaze dropped to Brady, the beloved dog, seated at his former master's side, leaning against him, his own gaze drifted to Alice before the k9 slid to the floor with a sigh.

Alice padded over to the resting dog and lovingly scratched at his scruff. "I think he misses having Samson around. Especially in the evenings."

"Probably." Sarah Sue glanced wistfully at the beloved dog. "But Samson's doing really well at his forever home." Turning her attention back to Alice, Preston's wife grinned widely. "Maybe it's time to take on another foster."

Laughing quietly, Alice shook her head at her daughter-in-law. "I don't know about that, but I'm pooped. And morning comes early on a ranch. I'm heading off to bed." With a final, tired smile, she blew a kiss to no one in particular, turned, and disappeared up the stairs.

Not wanting to see the contentment of the moment end just yet, Blake sank into the only empty chair in the room.

"I gotta admit…" Carson bobbed his head at Blake. Only two years younger than Kade, he spent a great deal of time with his older brother and his best friend. "It's nice to have you around. Even if you are mooching."

Kicking his head back, Blake let out a roar of laughter from deep in his gut. Somehow he'd forgotten that the Sweet family men were like his own brothers—they did not cut a man undeserved slack. "If I'd known how much I was missed, I'd have made more of an effort."

"Now don't get carried away." Biting back her own laughter, Rachel raised an open palmed hand to him. "You weren't missed *that* much."

Oh how he'd missed being part of this big raucous family. In some ways, the band and crew were his family now, but it was never anything close to this family. Heaving a sigh, he lifted his gaze to catch Rachel's eye. "I hope y'all understand how very sorry I am that I missed your dad's funeral. If it had been at all humanly possible, I would have been here."

Every Sweet in the room gave a short nod.

"We know." Preston tried for a smile.

"So tell me," he shifted in his seat, doing his best to lighten the mood, "who spiked the water?"

"Excuse me?" Jillian's eyes rounded in confusion. Pretty eyes.

"All these weddings in just a few months. Was it Miss Alice? Love potion number nine?"

"Ha." Jillian's shoulders shook with laughter. "Only a musician would come up with that one."

He couldn't help but grin. She appeared to be the only one in the room who got the joke of the old hit from the 1960s. There also weren't the words to express how deeply he regretted missing so many milestones in his friends' lives. Sadly, not till this very minute did he realize just how cavernous that regret was.

"Well…" Jillian was the one to clear her throat, but

somehow he got the impression that pretty much everyone in the room shifted uncomfortably. For just a flash of a second, he wondered if maybe someone *had* concocted a love potion. What was he missing?

"So," dropping his booted heel to the floor, Preston leaned forward, "what's the plan now with your grandmother? Are you really going to stay for as long as it takes to get a diagnosis?"

That was what he'd said, and whether his manager and record label liked it or not, that was his plan. "Yeah. That's exactly what I intend to do, though I can't very well hide out here forever."

Jillian stood and crossed the room, setting her hand on his shoulder. "I speak for all of us when I say you can hide out here as long as you want."

If he hadn't been so startled by the heat emanating from her fingertips, he would have said a heartfelt thank you. As it was he could barely manage a nod.

"At least your parents have agreed to cooperate with getting your grandmother to see a doctor." Jillian took a seat beside him. "That can go a long way."

"Sadly, I've dealt with families who have loved ones afflicted with dementia." Rachel shook her head. "The ones closest to the family member are often the hardest to convince that something is off. That their memory lapses aren't simply a factor of aging. Not until things start going seriously south."

"How seriously south?" It hadn't occurred to Blake that being a social worker, Rachel might know something about dementia.

"Anything from wandering out the door and not remembering how to come home, or thinking nine in the morning is nine at night."

Jillian gasped, her delicate fingers rising to cover her open mouth. This was exactly what had happened to his grandmother. She'd thought four in the morning was four in the afternoon.

Blake sighed, running a hand through his hair. "It's all so frustrating."

A little more conversation continued about his intentions for calling doctors, starting with Sarah Sue's dad. Preston's wife convinced him that having her father as an advocate would be a big help, and having known Doc Conroy all his life, Blake knew she was right. Quickly the conversation dwindled, filled now with yawns and stretching, Jess already having taken her and Carson's son to bed. One by one, couples began to wish each other goodnight. Preston and Sarah Sue headed off to their bunkhouse, then Garret muttered a goodnight to everyone as he slipped out the back door, presumably to the blue cottage.

Finally, only Jillian remained. "Follow me. I'll show you to your room."

Jillian stopped at the door across from the master bedroom. Kade's old room. The one where he and his best friend had spent countless hours plotting teenage mischief.

She gestured inside. "Mom set out fresh towels for you on the bed." Her gaze met his, and for a split second, the air between them thickened. The easy, friendly smile she'd been wearing all evening faltered, replaced by something unreadable, a flicker of vulnerability. He had to blink and take a step back. This strong, beautiful woman, willing to take on would be burglars, now partnering to solve all his problems and keep him comfortable. Who knew that little Jillian with her wide-eyed youthful wonder would turn out to be so…perfect?

CHAPTER SIX

"Where the hell are you?" That would be the third time in as many hours that Blake's manager sent him a text. The man had tried calling once or twice yesterday, and again today. Apparently now he'd opted to blow up Blake's phone. Only he wasn't ready to tell Phil where he was or why he was here. Not yet. That was just one thing he had to work out. If taking care of his grandmother meant canceling the upcoming European tour, he didn't want to think of the media firestorm that would create—not to mention the hit it would mean to his band members and road crew's wallet.

Tired of staring at the ceiling of Kade's old room, finding faces and figures in the popcorn texture, sitting up made more sense than continuing to toss and turn. The digital clock on the nightstand glowed 2:47 AM, mocking his restlessness.

What he needed was a cold drink, his guitar, and to sit on the back porch like he would when he and Kade were kids. The best music always came to him on the Sweet Ranch, maybe he'd find the peace he needed there as well.

Padding barefoot down the familiar staircase, a sliver of light caught his attention. Charlie Sweet's office door stood slightly ajar, warm lamplight spilling into the hallway. Blake hesitated. The last thing he wanted was to intrude, but something about the late hour and the solitary light tugged at his curiosity. He approached quietly and peered through the crack.

Hunched over the desk, Preston stared at the computer screen. Stacks of papers were scattered around him, some piled higher than others. Even from the doorway, Blake could see the tension in his friend's shoulders. Part of him thought it prudent to step back and leave the man to his work, another part of him considered the late hour and the deep frown etched between Preston's brows. Friends didn't abandon friends.

Gently, Blake rapped at the door.

Preston's face lifted, his eyes tired. "Hey, man. What has you up at this hour?"

"I could ask you the same." Blake inched into the room.

Tossing a pen on the desk, Preston rubbed his eyes and leaned back in the desk chair.

"No offense, but you look like hell." Blake sank into the leather chair across from the desk, the same spot where he'd sat countless times as a kid when Charlie Sweet had dispensed advice and reproof in equal measure.

"It's been a tough year."

A decade or so ago, he would have jumped right in and peppered his friend's brother with questions, but those days when they were all as thick as proverbial thieves were long gone. "How long have you and Sarah Sue been married now?"

A light shone in his eyes. Whatever had given him a rough time clearly wasn't his wife. "Not long enough."

Wow, that was not the answer he expected.

"I'm afraid our problems have nothing to do with Sarah Sue. Well," he chuckled, "unless you count her marrying me for money."

Blake blinked. "Say again?"

"Sorry." For the next while, without any hesitation, still treating Blake like one of the family, Preston explained how after Charlie Sweet passed, their old foreman Ray swindled his family of anything that wasn't nailed down along with all the money their dad had borrowed to take the ranch to the next level.

The sum of which had Blake's mouth going dry. "Ouch."

"Yeah, that about covers it. We were literally days from foreclosure." Preston continued to explain about the trust fund and how Sarah Sue stepped up to save the day.

"Holy Christmas. How did I not know y'all were trust fund brats?"

"We're not really. What we've been doing is scrambling to save the ranch."

Blake blinked, processing this information. "Wait. So all these recent weddings…"

"Weren't exactly coincidental," Preston confirmed. "Sarah Sue, Jess, Jackie—they all married into the family knowing it was a business arrangement. At least initially."

"Hold up." Blake leaned forward, his voice rising slightly, everyone looked so very happy and so very much in love—how could they be acting? "Y'all are just pretending?"

"Not at all. We all fell fast and hard."

Now that made way more sense than any pretense.

"The thing is, that makes it tough for Jillian," Preston continued.

"Tough?" Blake's gaze narrowed.

Looking at Blake, Preston paused, almost seemed to be sizing him up. "We're still not out of the woods so," he shrugged, "it's Jillian's turn. And eventually Kade will need to help out. Once the year is over for each marriage and we get the larger lump sums, we should be golden."

"But first, Jillian and Kade need to marry for money." It wasn't really a question.

Preston's face folded into a grimace. "Yeah, that about sums it up."

This was insane. Blake had to be dreaming. How could everyone in this family marry for business? This was the kind of craziness you'd see in a bad rom-com movie. "And if they don't get married?"

Preston's silence was all the answer Blake needed.

Running a hand through his hair, he tried to wrap his mind around it all. The Sweet family had always been his sanctuary, his second home when his own felt too small or too complicated. The idea that they were struggling didn't compute. Images of young Jillian, a bright eyed and curious kid, hiding by the porch, watching him tinker on his guitar popped into his head—the thought that this now grown woman might be pressured into marriage for money, made something fierce and protective rise in his chest. "There's got to be another way."

"We've explored every option." Preston's voice was flat with exhaustion. "Believe me."

Just then, the soft padding of footsteps outside the office, followed by a slight creak of the door, made both men look up. Jillian stood in the doorway, her eyes wide, dressed in a soft nightshirt, clearly unable to sleep either. She took in the scene—Preston, the papers, and him—and her gaze settled on Blake, a question in her eyes mirrored the chaos now churning in his own mind.

"Are we having a party?" In an effort to hide her exhaustion from tossing and turning, Jillian took a stab at lighthearted.

"Seems no one is sleeping tonight." Preston closed the lid on the laptop and heaved a deep sigh. "I was just catching Blake up on the challenges the ranch has had this year."

"Oh?" She felt her brows arch.

Preston nodded, then pushed to his feet. "I'm dead and too dumb to fall over. You two will have to entertain each other."

Jillian's cheeks warmed as thoughts of how to entertain each other flashed inappropriately in front of her.

From the way Blake sank a little lower in his seat, she wondered if his mind had taken a similar turn. "I was on my way to the kitchen for a drink."

"Me too." Jillian inched backward. Her intention had been not for a drink but to dive into a container of whatever ice cream called to her.

The three of them shuffled out of the room, Preston turning at the staircase and working his way upstairs, she and Blake made their way to the kitchen.

"What would you like?" Jillian pulled two bowls out of the cupboard.

Blake walked to the opposite cupboard, a small smile tugging at the corners of his mouth when he discovered like his grandmother's house, things were in the same place they'd been for ages. "Just some water."

Her head in the freezer, she moved the contents about, pulling out a container in each hand and holding them out to show their guest. "I have vanilla and butter pecan."

The slight smile widened to a full grin. "Butter pecan."

They walked back and forth past each other, Blake retrieving silverware from the drawer and napkins from the counter. Jillian stocked up with whipped cream, syrup toppings, maraschino cherry jar, and some chopped nuts.

His gaze following her from the fridge to table, their eyes met and Jillian shrugged, setting the ingredients on the table. "Hey, if we're going to do it, we might as well do it right."

This time, his brows rose high on his forehead and she realized how what she'd said sounded. This time there was no doubt where their minds had wandered. Immediately, her cheeks flushed with heat again.

Blake's smile bloomed impossibly wider. "You're cute when you blush. I don't remember you blushing much as a kid."

At ten she was too dang young to understand anything about sex and double entendres. Not sure what she could possibly say, she opted to shrug and dig into the frozen container of butter pecan ice cream. Doling two large scoops into a bowl, she lifted her gaze to meet his. "More?"

He shook his head. "No, that's plenty."

She slid the bowl in front of him and filled her own bowl as he smothered his cold confection in whipped cream and marshmallow syrup.

Not to be shown up, she added twice as much whipped cream and nuts as well.

Together, they ate silently for a few minutes, when Blake stabbed his spoon into the mound of melting ice cream and looked up at her. "Are you really going to get married for the trust?"

Unable to meet his gaze, she stirred at the whipped

cream. "That's the plan."

"Who?"

She dared lift her eyes to meet his. "Who?"

"Who are you going to marry for money instead of love?"

"It's not like that." She stabbed at the dessert again. "It's a business deal. A marriage of convenience." She lifted her chin and leveled her gaze with his. "In name only."

He actually scoffed. "Right. Like any man would be willing to marry you and stay out of your bed."

His tone was so bitter, she couldn't decide if that was an insult or a compliment.

"Sorry." He sighed and let his spoon rest in the bowl. "It's not my business, and certainly not my place to judge."

She didn't know why, but it really bothered her that he might think less of her because of what she had to do to help the family save the ranch. "It's complicated. There are a lot of conditions. Finding an agreeable male is only half the problem. My mother also has to believe that I've fallen head over boot heels in love and can't wait to marry my soul mate."

"So your mother doesn't know?"

"Absolutely not. She'd never agree to a stunt like this. Not even to save the ranch."

Under his breath, she was pretty sure he'd muttered something like *smart woman*.

"With Preston it was easy because Sarah Sue had been a neighbor and friend all of our lives. Carson had a son in college so that one was a no-brainer. Garrett was a little weird because he met Jackie in a bar, but apparently Mom is a romantic who believes in love at first sight. And of course, like Preston and Sarah, Rachel and Jim had been the brunt of town gossip in their youth which made it easy to believe they'd come to their senses."

"Is that what it's called nowadays? Coming to your senses?" Blake shook his head. "Sorry, forget I said that. You're right. You're all right. This ranch is worth saving, no matter the cost."

"Thank you." She didn't know why, but it mattered to

her that he understood and didn't judge.

His phone dinged, and Blake rolled his eyes.

"Something wrong?"

Blake shook his head. "Not really. Apparently, my manager doesn't believe in sleeping either."

"Oh." She watched him closely as he glanced at his phone, and grinding his teeth, turned the thing off. Apparently, he had more problems to deal with than just a forgetful grandmother. Wasn't life just peachy all around?

CHAPTER SEVEN

lake surveyed the long table Alice Sweet had set up on the back porch. Dressed in gingham and good intentions, the table looked more than inviting. The entire setting soothed like a balm to the soul, he only hoped Mrs. Sweet's plan of inviting his grandmother and Doc Conroy to lunch at the same time worked. Abreast of the situation, the town doctor had easily agreed to a little subterfuge over lunch. There really wasn't any other way Blake could think of to get his stubborn grandmother to see a doctor.

A pitcher of sweet tea, the kind strong enough to put hair on a mule and only a good Texan could appreciate, rested center stage along with a fresh batch of Miss Alice's cornbread muffins. Jillian had phoned him twenty minutes ago that she'd picked up his grandmother and should be here shortly.

Chuckling, Doc Conroy came from the kitchen carrying a platter of fried chicken. A few steps behind, Miss Alice cradled a massive bowl of potato salad, while sharing the tail end of a story about Mr. Sweet, a new foal, an over-protective mare, and the hole in his beloved lucky Stetson.

The sound of car doors slamming in the distance alerted Blake to the arrival of his best friend's little sister and his grandmother. The show was about to begin.

An hour later, their bellies full and their hearts merry with story after story of Blake's childhood and the Sweets adventures, Doc continued to keep a close eye on Sara Kirby.

"Sara," Doc smiled at the older woman, "do you remember what Abigail Fine said was the secret ingredient in her apple pie?"

"I do," his grandmother beamed, "and if I shared, it wouldn't be a secret anymore."

That made the doctor grin. "You always did have a memory like an elephant. I bet, if I gave you three words to remember, you'd have no trouble recalling them later on."

"Of course not."

"Okay. Let's see if everyone is as good as you." He turned to Alice. "Football, daisy, shoe. Think about those words, remember them, and repeat when I ask you."

Alice sweet softly mouthed the three words and nodded.

Doc did the same with everyone at the table, giving Sara Kirby the words house, bird, and puppet. The conversation circled around apple pie recipes when Doc looked at Blake's grandmother. "What were your three words, Sara?"

Grinning like the Cheshire cat, Sara proudly straightened her shoulders and easily repeated, "House, bird, and …" her smile slipped and her brows buckled. "It's on the tip of my tongue."

"No worries." Doc's smile remained in place. "Was it a child's toy?"

"Oh, yes," Sara brightened, "a marionette."

Everyone glanced at each other. Blake had no idea if using a synonym for puppet counted or not.

"Alice," Doc looked to his hostess, "I want to write this potato salad recipe down. May I have a sheet of paper?"

"Of course." In on the disguised tests, Alice Sweet jumped up and conveniently found a sheet of paper and a pen waiting at the counter just inside the door.

Doc scribbled a few things and then slid the paper to his side between him and Sara, pushed to his feet, and halfway to the kitchen door, turned to the older woman grinning at her grandson. "Sara, I don't want to lose that paper. Would you please fold it in half then set it on my seat? I'll get it when I come back from inside."

"You don't want me to leave it on the table?"

He shook his head. "I might forget it."

The older woman shrugged, reached for the sheet of

paper, folded it carefully in half, pressed the edge neatly, but instead of placing it on the seat as asked, set it on the table where the doc had sat. That much, Blake was positive, was not a good sign.

Stories continued to flow. Preston and Carson, who had joined them for lunch, pushed away from the table in an almost synchronized move. Despite the tension coiling in his gut at this casual lunch that was anything but, Blake couldn't help but smile at the brothers. All the Sweet boys, now men, were so different and yet, in many ways, so much alike. Their love for the land, their heritage, and each other, topped the list.

"I've got to get back to work," Carson said first.

Preston nodded. "Ditto." His wife trotting up the back steps, giving her father a kiss on the cheek and then turning to her husband, eyes sparkling, gave him a slower, sweeter peck on the lips. The not so private moment held Blake's rapt attention. How had all these siblings signed up for a business deal and wound up so in love even a blind man could see it?

"Sorry I'm late." Sarah Sue stepped away from her husband. "There was a situation with a placement I recently made. Had to unravel that mess."

"Oh, dear." Alice Sweet's face crumpled with concern.

"It's all fixed now, but it seems to be getting more and more difficult to place dogs right now. Everyone is tightening their belts and their budgets."

The way Miss Alice sighed, Blake had the feeling this wasn't the first time the family had held this conversation.

Once all those who had to return to work had left, the conversation shifted to Garrett and his students.

"You'd be amazed how much children struggle now reading a clock face." Doc casually interjected and everyone knew this was the next test. "We can all draw clocks, but today's kids, everything is digital."

Immediately, Ms. Alice retrieved a sheet of paper from the stack she'd brought to the table earlier, and doodled a face clock. "Is this what you mean?"

The doc seemed to study it as if imbedded on the page

were the winning lottery numbers. "Exactly."

"You try it." Ms. Alice slid a page to her daughter, then to his grandmother. Within minutes, as hoped, Sara Kirby had doodled a clock face, slowly, but accurately. Blake felt a slip of relief, …but not enough.

Lunch had gone much more smoothly than Jillian had expected. Even though she had the utmost confidence in Doc Conroy, she'd still had her doubts that Mrs. Kirby would cooperate so easily. She should never have doubted the doc.

With the family scattered back to their respective work, Mrs. Kirby cheerfully sat in one of the rockers, sharing a long-winded tale with Jillian's mom about a prize-winning rooster and a lovesick hen. In the meantime, Blake, the doc, and Jillian took advantage of the two women happily laughing and chatting to clear a few plates and empty tea glasses and carried them inside where the doctor could update Blake on his findings.

"Am I crazy?" were the first words Blake spit out before setting the dirty dishes on the counter.

Heaving a deep sigh, Doc shook his head. "I don't think so. I would have preferred to see her remember all three words on her own without prompting. Combine that with her forgetting the second half of the paper folding instructions, and I'd feel pretty confident in saying that Sara is indeed in the early stages of dementia."

"Alzheimer's?" Blake's gaze had narrowed and his voice had dropped to a near whisper.

Not wanting to intrude on the private conversation, Jillian inched toward the back door.

"No." Blake grabbed her hand. "Stay. Please."

Jillian nodded and they both turned to Preston's father-in-law.

"Maybe, maybe not," Doc continued. "She's going to need more tests and even then, it's pretty much a guess if it's Alzheimer's or any other forms of dementia. I'm going to call a friend of mine in Miller's Creek. He's a neurologist specializing in memory loss."

"I want the best." Blake shoved his hands into his pockets.

"I know son. Dr. Crawford is top in his field and going to Miller's Creek will be much easier on your grandmother than hauling her all the way to Dallas."

His lips pressed into a fine line, Blake nodded.

The doc grabbed his little black bag, a throwback to the days when even city doctors made house calls, and nodded at them both. "We'll see what Dr. Crawford has to say and move forward from there."

Blake and the doc shook hands. Doc Conroy stuck his neck out the back door to say goodbye, and the kitchen all sorted out, the two of them returned to the porch. Somewhere between gathering up the dirty dishes and saying goodbye to the doc, Jillian's mom had turned her phone on. Both women tapping the wooden floorboards to the tune of a familiar country song. Across from her, Blake stared off into the distance. She'd give anything to know what he was thinking, and what, if anything, she could do to help.

Taking a chance, she stood beside him, leaning against the porch railing as Sara and Alice sang loudly about friends in low places. "You didn't get your voice from your grandmother," Jillian teased.

As she'd hoped, the taunt brought a smile to his lips. "Poor Grams. Loves to sing, can't carry a tune in a paper bag."

A low squeal that should have been a note, made them both chuckle more heavily.

The opening notes of a familiar song filled the afternoon air, bringing her giggles to a stop. Blake's voice, smooth and achingly familiar, began singing "Honeysuckle Memories."

Blake froze, his expression shifting from surprise to something almost vulnerable.

"Oh my stars." Mrs. Kirby clapped her hands together

and leaned forward in her rocker. "It's you, Blake." Leaning back with a smile as wide as her face, the older woman set the rocker in motion. "I just love hearing you on the radio, but this is a new song."

His gaze locked on something in the distance, Blake only nodded.

Sara pushed to her feet, and crossing the short distance to the railing, tugged her grandson beside her. "Where are your manners? A good song comes on and a boy should always ask his grandmother to dance."

A smile, sweet, soft, and shaky, tugged at Blake's lips. "Of course. May I?" Bowing at the waist, she waved an arm across in a wide gesture.

The song only halfway through, Sara Kirby sucked in a deep breath and took a step back. "I'm getting too old to make it through an entire song." Stretching her arm, she snatched Jillian's hand, tugged her into the space by Blake and took a step back.

Blake raised his brows, a silent question, seeking approval. She put on a smile and nodded, stepping into his embrace, and a small piece of heaven. Lost in the moment, she almost leaped backward when the phone in her pocket buzzed against her hip.

When the song came to an end, Sara Kirby popped up from her seat with a great deal more energy than Jillian would have expected after her confession of being too old to dance, and applauded loudly. Still holding her hand, Blake took a bow and smiled at his grandmother, then her, before letting go of her hand.

Mourning the end of the song, she took a few steps back, leaned against the far wall, and searched her phone.

Her mother and Mrs. Kirby singing along to another tune, she felt, more than heard, Blake come stand beside her. "Anything wrong?"

"Hmm?" She glanced up at him.

"You're frowning."

"Oh, no. Not really."

"No, or not really?" His brows rose high on his forehead and his head tipped just slightly to the side.

"No," she clarified. Just because she was enjoying having Blake around didn't mean that a text from candidate number seven was a bad thing. So why didn't she want to tell Blake that she was one step closer to finding a temporary husband?

CHAPTER EIGHT

Dinner was barely over when Alice Sweet folded her napkin with purpose. "I think I'll ride down to the bunkhouse tonight. Picked up some new curtains in town yesterday for Clint's quarters."

A beat passed.

"You're putting curtains in the bunkhouse?" Rachel blinked.

Carson muttered something under his breath that sounded something like, *just what the man needs*. A sweet but reproving smile on her face, his wife elbowed him.

Their mother shot Carson a frosty glare, making them all feel five years old again. "The man works harder than any of us. I can't pay him more than pocket money. The least I can do is make his home a little nicer. Besides, the fabric was on sale and Liz sewed them for me."

"Tell me there are no rhinestones or sequins on them." Garrett's mouth puckered as if he'd sucked on a lemon.

Alice Sweet rolled her eyes heavenward. "Tell me, Charlie, when did our kids become such wise acres?"

Garrett held his hands up, palms out. "Sorry, Mom. But Aunt Liz does sell an awful lot of bling in her store."

"Selling it and making it for a ranch hand are two different things and would require an extra kind of stupid— and your aunts are not stupid."

"My apologies." Garrett glanced upward momentarily, as he extended his regrets to both parents.

Blake watched the exchange with a smile tugging at his lips. He missed the good-natured ribbing of a loving family.

With Alice out the door, as soon as the sound of her horse's hooves faded into the distance, Preston set down the dish towel he'd been using. "Dad's office. Now."

A collective sigh seemed to ripple through the room. The transition from family dinner to family pow-wow was seamless. Blake hung back, picking up a dish towel to finish where Preston left off.

"You might as well join us." Preston tipped his head in the direction of their dad's office. "You know as much as I do at the moment."

Feeling a bit like a fifth wheel, Blake hesitated. As much as he felt a part of this family all those years ago, for something of this magnitude, he felt like an interloper.

"We promise not to bite." Jillian smiled at him and nudged him forward. Had she said anything else, he wouldn't have guessed she recognized his discomfort. Had the kid always been that intuitive?

Blake followed the siblings down the hall, Brady padding along behind them.

Preston settled behind the desk, papers already spread out in front of him. The rest of them found seats, a few sank onto throw pillows on the floor—a full house. Blake leaned against the doorframe.

"I've been running the numbers most of the night," Preston began without preamble. "We've got funds for the next thirty days, maybe a week more if the ranch keeps producing profits. But then we're going to be scrambling again."

Jim leaned forward in his chair. "If we can hang on a few more weeks, bonuses will be distributed and I can—"

"If you two are going to build on Sweet land, you need to keep those bonuses," Preston interrupted. "What we need is more marriage money."

Blake felt his jaw tighten. These people—his second family—were talking about marriage like a business transaction. Again.

"Actually," Jillian said quietly, "I may have some news on that front. One of the guys I've been corresponding with online has agreed to the arrangement."

"Online?" Blake's voice came out sharper than he intended.

Jillian's cheeks flushed slightly. "It's not like there's a long line of eligible bachelors in Honeysuckle willing to enter into a marriage of convenience. Especially without letting on to Mom."

"What are his terms?" Preston leaned forward on his elbows.

"Standard arrangement. Marriage, wait out the year, divorce." Jillian paused, then blew out a short frustrated breath. "But he wants seed money after the divorce—quite a bit more than we'd planned for—in order to start his life over again."

A cold dread settled in Blake's stomach. He pictured the slimy types who'd prey on vulnerabilities. He gritted his teeth and pushed away from the doorframe. "Start his life over again? What is he, an ex-con?"

"Blake—" Jillian started.

"No, seriously. Who needs seed money to 'start over' unless they've got a record or massive debt or—"

The room erupted in overlapping conversations—peppering Jillian with questions from the practical where does he live, what does he do, to the more ridiculous, is he dying or sick? Garret, the only sensible one, was suggesting a background check while Preston spouted numbers and timelines.

Blake looked around the room. Staring up at him, head resting on his paws, even Brady seemed to have an opinion. The dog's one eyebrow was cocked higher than the other as if asking what was he waiting for.

Finally, Blake stuck his fingers in his mouth and let out an ear-piercing whistle. The room fell silent. "Y'all know this is totally nuts, right?" His gaze darted to each family member in the room.

Jillian shifted in her seat. "It's probably not as awful as it sounds. Chet—"

"Chet?" Preston frowned. "What kind of name is that?"

Shaking her head, Jillian stared at her older brother. "What difference does it make? Other than wanting money to leave, he seems pretty normal."

"Seems? Are you people listening to yourselves?" Even

constantly on the road in his crazy music world, Blake had never felt so out of touch with reality in his life. This just had to be a dream—or a nightmare.

"It could work out." Whether Rachel was trying to convince herself or the rest of her family, he didn't have a clue.

Blake felt his own jaw clench. He knew—or at least had known—the Sweets as well if not better than his own family, and understood the weight on their shoulders. The dog was right, he had to do something. "I have some cash I don't need. This place was my second home, practically. It's the least I can do."

"We're not asking for charity." Jillian's chin jetted out in indignation.

Charity was not good, but marrying a stranger in it for money was? Some things, like why the sky is blue and bears sleep in the winter, were simply not meant for him to understand. "Fine. I'll do it."

The room went dead silent.

"You'll what?" Jillian's soft voice was almost inaudible.

Blake ran a hand through his hair. "Marry me. I'm on the road most of the time anyway. It'll be a believable reason for a divorce in a year. I won't take your money. I'm not a criminal, and other than what we're about to do, I'm not insane. Besides, it will make it easier to check on Grams. Problems solved." Until someone figured out what was going on and had him committed.

Jillian stared at Blake. Snapping her mouth shut, she did her best to process what was going on in the room.

"This is serious." Rachel stared sternly at Blake. "Do you realize what you're agreeing to? Marrying Jillian, convincing the entire town—and our mother—that this is real."

"You're a public figure," Preston added. "Could this

have ramifications for you?"

For him? Jillian's mouth had gone dry. She couldn't decide what was worse, being married to a stranger who could be a complete psycho as easily as the perfect match, or Blake Kirby, the famous country singer and the one guy she'd had a schoolgirl crush on since she was, well, a schoolgirl.

"Trust me. I think I understand how serious being taken advantage of for your money is more than any of you." Blake crossed his arms. "Unless someone has a better idea than marrying a deadbeat."

"In all fairness," Carson leaned forward, "we don't know if this Chet character is a deadbeat or a godsend, but if we're taking votes, I'd trust Kirby with my sister any day of the week."

Heads nodded and Jillian's breath caught in her chest. A million things ran through her mind. All of which sent skitters up her spine and made her palms sweat.

Now lying at her side, his head resting on his paws, Brady's ears suddenly snapped to attention, followed by a low muttered woof. Thankful for something to do with her hands until her mouth could form words, Jillian leaned over the side of her chair and scratched the scruff of his neck. A moment later, the dog lifted his head and stared at a distant point, focusing on something none of them could hear.

"Brady?" Preston glanced at the dog. "What is it, boy?"

"Probably just Mom coming back." Carson shrugged, though he was carefully eyeing where Brady focused.

Another moment and the dog went from lying on the floor to sitting upright, and offering a low deep bark.

"That's not his Alice is home bark." Sarah Sue echoed Jillian's thoughts.

Suddenly Brady was on his feet, spinning in circles like a puppy. He raced to the office doorway. Without looking back at his family, the animal bolted down the hallway toward the front hall. The sounds of him jumping up at the door, scratching, and barking filled the house.

"What the hell?" Preston pushed back from the desk.

Every person in the room was on their feet, no doubt

fearing the worst, like the day that Brady had led them to their mother trapped on a barbed wire fence.

The sound of gravel crunching under tires drifted through the open windows, followed by a car door slamming. Brady's barking intensified, mixed with whines and the dog swiping at the door with a fervor she'd never seen before.

"Brady, settle down!" Carson called, but the dog ignored him completely.

Heavy footsteps echoed on the front porch.

"Isn't anyone going to open the door and see who it is?" Rachel stood behind her siblings all gathered by the door, staring at the dog.

Before anyone would react, the door swung open and Brady pounced forward, his massive paws landing on broad shoulders.

"Hey there, Brady boy," Kade laughed, catching the dog and nearly stumbling backward. "Miss me?"

Every inch of the dog's body was wiggling with sheer delight.

"Holy moly," Carson whispered.

"Kade!" several voices shouted at once, each one dripping with surprise and delight.

Jillian felt tears spring to her eyes. Her big brother was home. Her big brother, who'd been gone for what felt like forever, who they worried about every single day, was standing in the front hall, grinning that same crooked grin he'd had for as long as she could remember.

The family converged on him in a mass of hugs and chaos. Jillian managed to get her arms around his neck. "What are you doing here?"

Before he could answer, he was peppered with more questions. "Why didn't you tell us you were coming?" "How long can you stay?" "Is anything wrong, you're not sick or something?"

"Hang on." Kade squatted to give Brady some more scratches. "I'm fine. I've got a temporary duty assignment starting next month, so I'm here for a little...." His voice trailed off as his eyes fell on Blake. "Holy, mother of

Moses. What the hell are you doing here?"

In an instant he and his childhood best friend were engulfed in a back-slapping hug with a few jabs and pokes tossed in. Both laughing, memories of just how inseparable they'd been growing up came crashing down.

"About bloody time you showed your face around here." Kade yanked his almost brother into another bone crushing hug.

"Hey," Carson patted Kade gently on the shoulder, "be careful. You don't want to break your new brother-in-law before the wedding."

Kade's expression shifted faster than the speed of light, the sparkle in his eyes giving way to a narrowed gaze. "My new *what*?"

Smart man that he was, Blake took a step in retreat—outside fist throwing distance—and flashed a toothy smile. "Surprise?"

CHAPTER NINE

It was silly of Alice to be bringing curtains to a bunkhouse, but with little financial resources and Clint sacrificing so much for the ranch, she just had to do something to show her appreciation. Especially since Ray had almost ruined the ranch, an honest man at her side was worth his weight in gold. Sliding off the horse, she closed her eyes and prayed that Clint was the man she thought him to be, then pulling the folded panels from her saddle bag, marched up to the door and knocked.

The old wooden door swung open and she didn't know who looked more surprised, Clint at finding her standing at his door, or her for finding him shirtless and barefoot. Any fool could see every muscle from his neck to his six-pack showed this man worked hard for a living. Probably always had. Not that six-pack abs would hold up in a court of law to prove Clint was an honest man, but it was enough for her. "I know it's late…"

"No." Running his fingers through his hair, Clint did his best to tame the unruly dark locks. "I was just watching television."

"I, uh, brought some curtains."

If she thought he'd been surprised a moment ago, wide circles of white surrounding deep blue eyes teetered on utter shock.

Maybe this hadn't been as good an idea as she'd thought.

Clint must have realized her discomfort. Pulling the door fully open, he stepped to one side and waved her in before hurrying to the sofa and shrugging into his shirt. Quickly gathering dirty dishes and empty wrappers from the small table in front of the couch, he shrugged. "Sorry for the mess. I wasn't expecting…company."

"Apologies are mine. I should have called."

Clint chuckled and swiped his hand through his hair again.

"Did I say something funny?"

Biting back a grin, the corners of his mouth tipped slightly upward anyhow, making his eyes sparkle. Honest eyes. "It's your ranch. You don't need to call to come to the bunkhouse. It's not like I'm entertaining or anything."

With the paltry amount of money she gave him, she doubted he could afford to feed a cat, never mind *entertain* a…person. "I apologize anyway, but if you don't mind, I thought it might brighten the place up a bit to hang curtains."

Looking up at the few windows in the room, his gaze darted back to her. "Of course."

Consumed by the muscles, the grin, and awkwardness of her surprise visit, not till this moment did she realize the bunkhouse looked different. Considering it was where cowboys hung their hats, the place looked almost… homey. The furniture had been moved around, and a few pieces that weren't hers had been added. An oversized comfy chair— what Charlie would have called a man's chair—faced a small television. A bookcase on the far wall held a scattering of framed photos and other knick-knacks. Definitely not a common sight in a bunkhouse intended to house a slew of men. The urge to cross the room and examine the photos was strong, but she resisted.

"I'll get a stepstool." Without waiting for her response, he darted off down the narrow hall.

Unfolding the curtains and leaning the tension rods under the first window, she grabbed a chair and dragged it in front of her first target. Hauling herself up, she balanced on the edges of the seat and slid the rod into the curtain. By the time Clint returned with the stepstool, the first curtain was in place and she was back on solid ground. By the time she'd hung the last curtain, she'd gotten close enough to see the photo of a much younger Clint and a young boy whose sparkling eyes bore a strong resemblance to his. Did Clint have a family? She'd never seen his application. Stealing a few more glances, no photos of a wife or mother of the boy, only him and the young child. Interesting. For the first time since finding out about swindling Ray, she realized just how little she knew about her one and only ranch hand.

Kade's gaze narrowed fiercely and Blake could only imagine the myriad of thoughts running through his head. Most of which would be the none too flattering events early in his career that involved women, parties, vats of alcohol, and of course, more women. But that had all been a long time ago.

"Reel it in, bro." This came from Preston, patting his older brother firmly on the shoulder. "Remember the trust money?"

Kade blinked, but continued to drill Blake with that big brother death ray gaze that all the Sweet men had developed around their little sisters.

"Would you rather she married Chet?" Carson flashed a toothy grin at their military brother.

"Chet?" Kade practically growled, spinning around to face his two brothers.

"That's the guy that answered Jillian's ad for a husband. Of course he wants money."

"Money?" Kade's jaw twitched from the pressure of grinding his teeth.

"Okay, boys." Rachel pushed between her two brothers and came to a stop in front of Kade. "Suck it up, buttercup. You know what we're all doing so quit with the macho big brother bit."

Now Kade's eyes rounded and he spun around to face Blake. "This is all just for show?"

Both he and Jillian nodded, but it took Blake a few seconds to find his words. "Chet didn't sit well with me either. I promised you I'd protect them and I meant it."

"You what?" Jillian spun around to face him.

Blake shrugged. "I meant it at the time. I just didn't expect my life to go the way it did. But I'm back now, at least for a short while, and I'm going to keep my word."

"Oh, my." The porch door slamming shut, their mother's eyes were big and round and her smile spread from ear to ear. Within seconds she bolted across the living room floor and had her eldest son swooped into a hug as if he once again was a little boy. "Why didn't you tell me you were coming? I would have made your favorite foods."

Those words made everyone smile.

"I wanted to surprise everyone." Kade held on tightly to his mother before the two finally separated.

Apparently, tonight was a night of surprises for everyone. But Kade had at least one thing right; Blake needed to assure everyone that his intentions were to help save the ranch, nothing more.

"I bet you're hungry." Alice Sweet stepped back and darted toward the kitchen. "It will only take a minute to warm up a plate for you."

"Thanks, Mom." Kade blew out an easy breath.

"Welcome home, bro." Garrett bumped shoulders with his brother.

Rachel followed her mother, Sarah Sue right behind her. "Let me help, Mom."

"Me too." Jillian darted after her sister and sister-in-law.

Kade turned, and lowering his voice, looked less viciously at Blake. "You really up to this?"

He could have been an ass and poked at his lifelong friend's lack of specifics, but now was not the time for that. All he did was nod. "As a matter of fact, I have a different show to put on. Excuse me."

Trying not to feel like he was walking the plank, Blake joined the women in the kitchen. Jillian had popped a few rolls into the oven to warm and he eased up beside her. Slowly, he eased his fingers through hers. "Can I talk my favorite tag along into a quiet walk outside?"

He knew full well that would catch her mother's

attention, but it took Jillian a few moments of surprise before understanding dawned and she nodded. "It's a nice night for a walk."

Still holding her hand, he led her to the back door, feeling Alice Sweet's gaze on his back with every step. He sure hoped he knew what he was getting into.

Everything about this evening felt oddly surreal. First having all her brothers under one roof was a blessing beyond measure. Now, walking hand in hand with her childhood crush, even if it was just for show, the world seemed to have either tilted on its axis or spun out of orbit and she didn't have a clue which one it might be.

"I hope you didn't mind, but I figured, if we're on a short timetable, then we need to figure out a few things and no offense, but your brother's breathing down my neck didn't seem like the right circumstances."

"Agreed." She hadn't decided what she thought of all this, or if she could even go through with it. Any of it. With Blake, or Chet, or anyone. Everything had worked out for her siblings, but odds of five out of five successful matches weren't encouraging.

His thumb began drawing swirls around the back of her hand and an odd sensation fluttered past her wrist and up her arm. "I don't quite know where to start."

"That makes two of us." Finally, she had a full sentence come to mind.

"It will take a little time to get Grams to the doctor in Miller's Creek, so I'll be here for that long, but there's a lot going on with the band and the next tour and I won't be able to put it all off for too long. Not without costing the company some serious money."

She bobbed her head. "I suppose you're having to leave to go back on tour would be a simple and legitimate reason for wanting to rush into marriage." At least she hoped so. If she went through with it.

"You're not sure, are you?"

She stopped in her tracks and turned to look at him for the first time since leaving the kitchen. "Right now, I'm not sure of much of anything."

"Were you more sure about Chet?" He continued walking.

Shaking her head, she heaved a short sigh. "No."

"Good." His smile stretched across his face. "I can't tell you why, but I don't like the man."

Tilting her head, she studied him more closely. Was this brotherly protective instincts, or was she reading something more into his reaction?

At the entrance to the barn, Blake paused and looked in the doorway. "Some folks might think me mad, but I've missed the smell of a stable."

A burst of laughter escaped. For the first time all evening, she felt relaxed and comfortable in her own skin. "You can take the boy out of Texas but you can't take Texas out of the boy."

Now he laughed. "I guess not."

"You're glad to be back, aren't you?" She wasn't sure why she stated the obvious, but she got the feeling he hadn't quite embraced how much home felt like home.

Looking over an open stall, he shifted his focus from the horse inside to her and let out a low huff. "I guess I really am." The horse nickered at him, and chuckling, Blake reached over and scratched the mare's neck, and she leaned into him. "That's my girl," he cooed.

Jillian had no idea how any of this had come to pass. What was she doing here with a famous rock star? What was he thinking agreeing to pretend marry her? "Are we really going to do this?" Hearing her words out loud surprised her.

Stepping back, nodding his head, Blake turned to her. "Yeah. I think we are."

The air grew thick, so thick she was sure if she waved her arms it would separate like the Red Sea. "We have to fool everyone. It's not just on paper. My mom, the town, the lawyers, the bank."

Again, Blake nodded. Stepping to the side, he took hold of her hand again, leaned forward, and whispered within a few inches of her, "Just for practice."

She'd barely processed the words when his lips pressed against hers. Softly, sweetly, so very tenderly. Then, before she could lean into the kiss, he pulled back and she had to resist the urge to touch her fingers to her tingling lips. There was one thing she was absolutely sure about... she had no idea what the heck she was getting into.

CHAPTER TEN

The morning after Kade's chaotic return, a surprising sense of calm had settled over the Sweet Ranch. As his mother had predicted, Kade was sleeping in, a small indulgence after years of military structure. Blake, however, felt a restless energy he couldn't shake. He needed to go to town, to see his grandmother, to tell her about the appointment Doc Conroy had arranged for her in a few days. It was an errand, but it felt like a mission, one small, concrete step forward in the mess of uncertainty.

Forgoing a second cup of coffee, he grabbed his keys from the bowl by the door. Alice Sweet intercepted him, her gaze swept from his baseball cap down to his designer boots and back up again. She shook her head with the same expression she'd worn when catching one of her boys trying to sneak a frog into Sunday service.

"Here." Handing him a well-worn cowboy hat hanging on a peg near the door, her tone left no room for argument. "This is Texas, Blake, not Yankee Stadium." She then nodded toward the window where his black rental SUV gleamed in the sun. "And for heaven's sake, take one of the ranch trucks. That shiny thing makes you stick out like the Secret Service. You might as well hang a banner across the back that shouts Blake Kirby is back in town. Though I don't understand why you being here has to be such a secret. This town takes care of its own, and like it or not, you're still one of ours."

"Yes, ma'am." A slow smile tugged at Blake's lips. There was no arguing with Alice Sweet's logic. Sliding his sunglasses into place, he swapped his usual baseball cap for the cowboy hat, the traditional accessory settling comfortably on his head. The parts about not needing to keep secrets and still being one of the town's own, he wasn't so sure about.

Driving down Main Street, he decided to stop at Heaven Scent first. The thought of seeing Jillian, even for a moment, was a stronger pull than he cared to admit. Pulling into an open spot in front, his phone beeped with another message from his manager, Phil. Did that man never give up?

Stepping away from the parked truck, he paused by the large plate glass window. Jillian stood behind the counter, her head bent over something. The little bell above the door chimed as he entered. The air inside filled with a warm, fragrant cloud of vanilla, lavender, and the distinctly popular Honeysuckle.

The scene playing out in front of the counter stopped him in his tracks. Not the candles, or the tantalizing aromas, but two little girls. Considering their matching golden locks and pink hair bows, he'd guess sisters. Both stood on tiptoes, their heads barely clearing the countertop. One had a small, determined hand planted on a pale yellow candle, the other had meticulously arranged a small pile of coins and crumpled dollar bills in front of Jillian.

"Our mama loves yellow roses," the older one announced with grave importance. "Tomorrow is her birthday. We want to give her this one."

Jillian leaned forward, her expression a perfect blend of sweetness and serious consideration. Blake watched, fascinated. This was a side of her he hadn't considered—not just a grown-up, but a business owner, a gentle pillar of her community.

"What a thoughtful gift. I'm sure your mama is going to love it." She made a show of carefully counting the pile of money, her lips moving silently. Then, with the solemnity of a bank teller, she picked out a quarter and pushed it back toward the girls. "And here's your change."

The girls' faces lit up like Christmas morning. "Really?" the one who'd been holding the candle asked.

"Really." Jillian's smile was nearly as bright as the two

little girls. "And since it's for your mama's birthday, I think we should wrap it up special, don't you?" She disappeared for a moment, returning with a small, cheerful gift bag and a cascade of tissue paper.

She wrapped the candle with a care and artistry that seemed far beyond the small transaction. Completely unbidden, a genuine smile spread across his face.

"There you go." She handed the bag to the girl who'd counted out the money. "I hope your mama loves it."

"She will!" both girls chorused, practically bouncing with excitement as they rushed past Blake without a second glance, their treasure clutched safely between them, already chattering about their mother's surprise.

Blake stood there for a moment, something shifting in his chest as he watched Jillian straighten the counter. Who knew that the quiet little kid who used to watch her brothers like they were a forbidden movie would grow up to be not only pretty and smart, but as sweet as her name? Of course those kids didn't have near enough money for the retail value of that candle, but that wasn't the point. Jillian was a good sport—no, she was more than that. She was kind in a way that came from the heart, not from obligation. Treating two little girls buying a candle for their mother as if they were her most important customers of the day. The contrast between her world and his suddenly became very illuminating.

"That was nice of you." He approached the counter.

Jillian looked up, startled. A soft pink crept up her cheeks. "I didn't see you come in."

"I was watching the master at work." He leaned against the counter, still smiling. "Something tells me those girls didn't have quite enough money for that candle."

Her blush deepened. "They had enough," she said quietly.

"For a three-dollar candle, maybe."

"It was a three-dollar candle." Her eyes twinkled.

Blake laughed, the sound surprising him. "Right. And I'm just a guy who plays a little guitar on weekends."

"Well," Jillian's lips twitched with suppressed laughter,

"you do play a little guitar."

And just like that, he knew returning to Honeysuckle had been the smartest move he'd made in a very long time—and that realization was just a little terrifying.

"You're home awfully early." Fingers deep in a blob of dough, Jillian's mother looked up from the kitchen table.

"Not a lot of tourists in town today. Carol can handle it on her own so I came home."

Her mother stared at her a long moment before pounding at the dough again. "Blake went into town today."

"Yeah."

Flipping the dough, her mother lifted her gaze to meet Jillian's. "Yeah, you saw him? Or yeah, someone told you?"

"I saw him."

"Mm." Her mom waited a beat, probably waiting for Jillian to expound. When nothing more was said, she sighed. "On the street? At his grandmother's? His parents?"

"At Heaven Scent. He came in…" Jillian paused—why had he come in? "To look around."

Before her mother could say much more than *Uh-huh*, the back door swung open. "Have you heard the latest?" Kade paused long enough to brush the muck from outdoors off his boots.

"Care to be more specific?" Her mother's searing glare shifted suddenly to wide eyes. "Is it about Ray and the ranch hands? Did you see the sheriff?"

Shoulders deflating on a heavy sigh, Kade shook his head. "Sorry, Mom. I haven't heard anything about that sniveling…" his teeth clenched. "It's about Blake."

"Blake?" Jillian's heart stuttered against her ribs. "Is he okay? Is it his grandmother?"

Holding his hands up, palms out, Kade shook his head. "As far as I know, his grandmother is fine, but according to his manager, Blake is missing."

"Missing?" Their mother looked up, her brows buckled

in confusion.

He held out his phone for them to see. "It's all over the news and social media. His manager, Phil, told reporters that Blake has not been seen since the end of the tour, and his whereabouts are unknown."

"What the…." Jillian looked at the phone, swiped at the screen, and then swiped again and again. Slowly raising her head, she blinked and handed her brother back his phone. "Is this a publicity stunt?"

"Has the whole world gone nuts?" Dropping his briefcase on the hutch, Garret walked into the kitchen. "Who knew seventh graders were so into Blake Kirby?"

"They saw him?" Jillian asked.

"No." Garret whipped out his phone. "He's all over the news, social media, and now there are short videos popping up everywhere of him just about any place you can imagine. Thanks to AI, he's getting around more than Carmen San Diego."

"Or Waldo." Kade shrugged.

"Hey," the screen door squeaked open, "have you guys heard…" Sarah Sue didn't get to finish her sentence.

"Looks like everyone has heard." Kade slipped his phone into his breast pocket.

While more siblings and their spouses made their way into the family kitchen, their voices creating a symphony of sound, Jillian wondered what all this would mean for Blake.

With just about every family member accounted for, when the front door swung open, all eyes turned to see the man himself walking into the house. At the dead silence that had struck, and everyone's attention on him, Blake stopped suddenly and glanced down at his feet. "Did I step in something?"

"That depends." Kade walked over to his friend and handed over his cell phone.

Blake's eyes grew wider with every swipe. "What the hell is Phil thinking?"

"That there's no such thing as bad publicity?" Her mother's tone dripped with enough sweetness to bake a cake.

Several voices began speaking all at once, but Jillian's gaze remained fixed on Blake. The way he scrolled through his own phone now, his lips pressed into a thin line, the muscle in his jaw almost twitching from the tension, his gaze narrowed and focused. Inching closer to him, she couldn't resist reaching out, letting her hand rest on his arm. Pleased when the tension in his shoulders eased the slightest bit, she stood there silently offering support.

When Blake heaved a sigh and placed his free hand on hers, still resting on him, the silent communication felt oddly comforting. At least to her.

His one hand still flicking at the phone, his other hand shifted, grasping her hand in his. That alone made her breath catch, but when he squeezed her hand before sliding the phone into his pocket, she thought her heart would pound its way out of her chest.

"I think I need to make a phone call." Blake eased away, his gaze on Jillian. "This won't take long."

All she could do was nod. As he stepped onto the back porch, her siblings still talking over each other, her gaze landed on her mother. From the way one arch rose higher than the other and her hands had stilled from their kneading, Jillian would guess her mom had been the only one in the room watching her and Blake's interactions.

What she couldn't figure out was why that seemed to bother her. The entire trust fund plan would only work if their mom believed each and every one of them was marrying for love not for money to save the ranch, and yet, knowing this, knowing that soon, very soon, she and Blake would have to start putting on a show, this felt very different, and all too real. And once again she had to ask herself if pretending with Blake wasn't the worst idea she'd ever had.

CHAPTER ELEVEN

"What the hell are you doing?" The screen door had barely slammed behind Blake when he punched in his manager's private number.

"So you remembered how to use a phone?" Phil Mercer could be so annoying some days.

"Never mind me. What's this I'm missing thing all about?"

"Hey, I had to find some way to flush you out. Apparently, it worked."

"You couldn't have just left a voice mail?" Blake leaned against the railing.

"I tried that. You didn't return my calls."

"I didn't have anything to say." Not yet, he wanted to figure out what was going on with his grandmother and he didn't want Phil telling him why he couldn't do that.

"The production company in London wants you fly in a week early."

"No."

"They want you to do a benefit concert for one of the king's favored charities and the week before the first concert is not only perfect timing, it will do a lot to help with sales when we release the live concert album."

"What part of no isn't clear?" Normally sarcasm wasn't typical for him, but he was really ticked off at what Phil had done to get his attention.

"Are you listening to me? I said *the king*."

"I heard you." No one was more important than his family. The thought caught him by surprise, but it was heartfelt and sincere. No matter the cost, his grandmother had to come first. "I need you to retract the statement to the press. The last thing I need is for every Tom, Dick, and reporter hunting me down like a rabid dog."

"I'll see what I can do, but you know how this sort of thing works. Putting the genie back in the bottle doesn't always work well."

"I don't care how you do it, just do it."

"Okay. And I'll let the team know that you'll do the concert."

"The answer is still no. My grandmother isn't well."

A long pause hung on the other end. Finally, Phil found his words. "Cancer?"

"No. She's confused."

Phil scoffed. "Blake, half the world is confused right now. Heck, probably more than that. I'm going to say yes."

"Do that and you're fired."

Another silence and Blake could almost feel the steam coming from Phil's ears right through the cell phone speaker. "You can't throw your career away because your grandmother can't remember when your birthday is."

So he did recall their conversation right after his grandmother's middle of the night birthday call. "Saying no to a benefit, or even canceling a concert if it comes to that, is not going to end my career."

"Wait. Canceling? Blake, I don't know what you've been smoking, but you need to get your head on straight. I'm going to let you sleep on it. I'll call you tomorrow. And next time, answer the damn phone."

Before Blake could respond, the line went dead. What Phil didn't seem to understand, and what Blake was becoming increasingly aware of, was that his head might very well be on straight for the first time in a long time.

"Everything okay?" Jillian stood in the back doorway, her hands on the screen door. She really grew up to be beautiful in so many ways.

"Not sure." Glancing down at his phone, he briefly wondered what stunt Phil might pull next, before footsteps from the house had him lifting his gaze to meet hers.

"That doesn't sound good." She came to a stop at his side, only instead of looking at him, or his phone, her eyes followed the stars sparkling in the sky like a diamond on velvet. "Something about the night sky that always makes me think nothing is insurmountable."

Taking a good long look, he realized it had been forever since he'd seen a sky like this. There was no room for argument. The Texas sky could make anyone and their problems seem small. "Are we talking about my problems, or your problems?"

Heaving in a deep sigh, she slowly blew out a long, easy breath. "Both, I guess." She spun around so her back was to the rail and the sky. "Are you sure you want to do this? Bail out my family?"

There was no need to think, he was already nodding his head.

"I snore." Her cheeks took on a pinker tone. "According to Rachel, like a chainsaw."

That had him laughing softly, quickly forgetting his own troubles. Without thinking, he lifted his hand and gently tucked a loose strand of hair behind her ear. "I'm a very sound sleeper. Once in LA, I slept through an earthquake. Woke up to find the kitchen cabinets had swung open and pretty much every glass and plate in the house was smashed on the floor."

"Good to know." Her smile was so dang sweet. Just like her name. "So, now what?"

He shrugged. "Y'all have done this four times already. Maybe you should tell me?"

"Well," her gaze darted to the house and back, "each one put on a show for Mom and the town, then quickly had an excuse to marry. The hard part was everyone had to live here under Mom's nose. Originally Preston and Sarah Sue thought they'd live in his apartment, but when it burned down and there became a shortage of housing, everyone had to live here."

Nodding, Blake thought about that. He didn't own a house here. Living with his parents or her parents was six of one or half a dozen of the other. Living under a microscope, at least while he was in town, wouldn't be easy. "Has the housing shortage improved any? I mean, could I buy a house for us?"

Her head shook from side to side. "Everyone displaced snatched up anything available. There isn't much property turnover in Honeysuckle, and Preston's apartment building is still under construction. Determining the cause as well as permit issues delayed the repairs. I heard there was a debate whether to refurbish or tear it down and start over."

"Who won?"

"The refurbish side. Though by the time it's done, there won't be much, if anything, original on the inside."

"So it sounds like we date, we get engaged, we marry, and at first, we live here?"

"That about covers it."

"How much time do we have to pull all this off?" He had a crazy urge to take her hand, or better yet, pull her into the fold of his arms. Not smart.

"Yesterday would have been good."

He sucked in a hiss of air. "That soon?"

This time her chin dipped in an affirmative gesture, but he could see from the way that she nibbled on her lower lip, she wasn't anymore comfortable with the timeline than he was.

Debating how he was going to pull off dating Jillian and keeping a low profile, he reached for her hand, and before he could fully process what he was doing, he'd pulled her into his personal space. Ignoring the squeak of the screen door hinges, leaning in, he pressed his lips ever so gently to hers.

There was no time to think. Her toes were curling and her arms looped around Blake's neck. Deepening the kiss, Blake slid his arms around her waist and eased her even closer. She had no idea what heaven would be like, but it couldn't possibly be better than wrapped in Blake's arms.

A throat cleared behind them. Maybe if she ignored whoever it was, they would simply go away. Once again, the throat cleared more loudly, followed by her mother's voice. "Excuse me."

Her mother? Dropping her arms to her side, Jillian sprang back faster than if someone had set her on fire.

Standing behind her daughter, Alice Sweet wore a smile that was almost as wide as her face. "Mildred McEntire called for you."

"What does Mildred need with me?" The kiss had Jillian's brain all fogged. She couldn't think of why the bling queen of Honeysuckle would need her.

Her mother shook her head. "Not you. Blake."

"Me?" The man's eyes rounded in surprise.

Before Alice could say anything more, high heels clacking against the wooden floors inside echoed loudly, the sound growing closer until the screen door flew open and hands on her hips, toes tapping, Iris Hathaway stood in the doorway. "You're going to have to figure something out. And fast. There are at least ten different reporters snooping around downtown."

"How did you know he was here?" Jillian blurted out.

Iris shot her a *you're-kidding* glare. "Blake, honey, if you think wearing a cowboy hat and not shaving would keep your presence in town a secret, you've got another *think* coming."

"Excuse me?"

"We figure you must have your reasons for not wanting anyone to know you're back home and hiding out at the Sweet Ranch, but you can't go slinking around town in a hoodie, climb into your grandmother's window, drive a flashy car out of town, and no one knows what you're up to."

"I, uh, see," Blake muttered softly.

Jillian felt her cheeks burn. The entire town had been watching Blake, and no one had said a word?

"Does the whole town know I'm here?" Blake ran a hand through his hair.

"Since about five minutes after you climbed through your grandmother's window," Iris said matter-of-factly. "Honey, this is Honeysuckle. A stranger can't sneeze downtown without half the town knowing about it by supper. You think a famous rock star can break into his own grandmother's house in broad daylight and we wouldn't notice?"

Alice stepped forward, her expression gentle. "The whole town's been protecting you, Blake. We figured you had your reasons for wanting privacy."

"But now we've got reporters sniffing around." Iris's voice took on a more urgent tone. "They're asking questions, showing pictures, offering money for information about where you are. It's only a matter of time before someone talks, whether they mean to or not."

"Pictures?" Blake asked.

"All kinds of photos. You with the band, you on stage, you with some blond in a strappy top, another with a redhead, uh, on, your lap. You know, typical rock star stuff."

"Hmm." Blake's gaze darted to Jillian and back, his fingers raking through his hair with more pressure. "Marvy. Just marvy."

Jillian's stomach dropped. It hadn't occurred to her how things were going to go this year with him on the road, supposedly married to her, and all the groupies hanging all over him. Knots formed in her stomach.

"What I don't understand is," Iris said, "why are you hiding out?"

"Trying to avoid exactly what's happening now. Paparazzi crawling all over town, bothering people, making sh…stuff up. They're always making stuff up. Like those photos of women." He turned to Jillian, leveling his eyes with hers. "There are no women in my life, not anymore. No groupies. Nothing. Those photos are either older than Moses or artificially generated—which, again, is why I wanted to keep paparazzi away."

"What kind of questions?" Jillian asked Iris, wanting to desperately believe what Blake was telling her.

"The usual." Iris shrugged. "Where you're staying, are you sick, are your parents sick, are you on a binge, do we think you've checked into rehab."

"Rehab?" He spun around, clenching his fists at his sides. "Where do they come up with this crap!"

"Hey," Iris held up her hands, "don't shoot the messenger."

Nudging Iris aside, Kade stepped forward, his expression grim. He looked from Blake to Jillian, then to the rest of his siblings who had slowly followed him onto the back porch. "She's right. We can't just hide him. This isn't a game; reporters don't give up, they dig. If we don't give them a story, they'll invent one. And theirs will be a hell of a lot worse than the truth."

"The truth?" Blake let out a humorless laugh. "The truth is I'm here because my grandmother is showing signs of dementia and I'm terrified. You think I want that splashed across the tabloids?"

The raw vulnerability in his voice squeezed at Jillian's heart. Without thinking, she reached over and grabbed his hand, squeezing it slightly, offering what little comfort she could. The slight tipping of one corner of his mouth as he squeezed back only confused her more.

Her mother moved to Blake's other side, as she'd done so many times, so many years ago. Her mother was there for all her children, and her sort-of children. "Of course not, dear."

"So what's the alternative?" Garret asked. "We stonewall them?"

"That'll just make them dig harder," Carson countered. "And with the reporters offering money to the locals for any gossip, it won't be pretty."

Jillian felt completely helpless. Now what?

Kade's focus narrowed, his gaze locking first on his sister, then on his one-time best friend. A glimmer of light dawned in his eyes, the look of a soldier assessing a battlefield and finally seeing a single, viable path forward. "We'll give them a story we all can live with. A different story. A better one. One they won't see coming."

Her brother looked to Blake, his gaze dropping to Jillian and his clasped hands, then back up. He waited a beat, staring at Blake until through some unspoken language.

Blake got the message and nodded his agreement.

Suddenly, Carson starting bobbing his head, a smile teasing his lips. "I get it. What we were discussing earlier?"

Kade nodded. "You came to visit family during your break. You met the girl you left behind—"

"If you mean me," Jillian had begun to put the pieces together, "I was ten the last time I saw Blake. If they're any kind of reporters, they'll figure that out fast."

"Agreed." Blake pulled Jillian closer to his side. "But you're on the right track. I reconnected with my best friend's little sister, who isn't so little anymore."

"Oh," Sarah Sue clapped her hands together, "everyone loves a best friend little sister story. The reporters are going to eat it up. So will your fans."

The air sizzled with an unexpected electricity.

Alice Sweet walked over and pulled her daughter into a tight hug. "I don't know what happened here, but I couldn't be happier for you." Her mom eased back and then gave Blake an equally warm embrace until her phone beeped and she sprang back. "Oh, heck. I forgot about Mildred. I'll tell her what's going on."

"And I," Iris turned to follow Alice, "will get started on spreading the word about the new romance." Rubbing her hands together, Iris almost shook with excitement as she hurried back into the house.

Preston turned to Blake. "I guess we've killed two birds with one stone. Your presence in town," he spun around to face the other siblings, "and our next trust fund payment is just a marriage license away."

CHAPTER TWELVE

The worn cowboy hat Alice had pressed on him the other day felt surprisingly natural, a low-profile disguise that, combined with the dusty ranch truck, should have been enough to dodge any unwanted attention—not that it had done any good hiding from the town, but it should be enough to avoid any lurking reporters. Just in case, Blake had left the ranch immediately after breakfast at zero dark thirty. Most of Main Street was still sleeping. Pulling into the lot at Miller's Dry Goods, he took a front parking space, figuring the best hiding place was right under everyone's noses. No one would expect him to show his face if he was hiding.

Adjusting the brim of his hat, he slipped on his sunglasses and headed down the cracked sidewalk toward his parents' street. Only a few blocks away, he opted to cut through the back alley. It was one thing to park out in the open in a grocery store parking lot, it was another to march up to his parents' front door for all to see. If Alice Sweet and Iris Hathaway were correct, by midday today the reporters would have their answers, a story to file and print, and be on their merry way back to any big city in search of some other seedy headline.

His plan was simple: slip into his parents' backyard, give them the story before they heard it from the town gossip mill, and slip back out. Somehow, calling to inform them that he was now dating Jillian Sweet and expected to marry her soon—very soon—felt wrong. Even if this was a business deal at heart, after all, the Sweets financial struggles were not his to share. But if he were going to make this feel real, he knew an announcement of this magnitude was something he'd tell them in person.

He vaulted the low wooden gate into his parents' yard, the same one he'd jumped a thousand times as a kid. The yard was empty, quiet. He crept up the back steps, his boots silent on the weathered wood, and peered through the screen door into the kitchen. His mom stood at the stove, his dad in his spot at the kitchen table. Perfect.

Inching the door open, his mother's face brightened instantly. "Blake." A moment later, he found himself in a bone crushing hug. Anyone would think she hadn't seen him in months or years, not just the other day.

"This is a surprise, son." His father wasn't the touchy feely sort that his mother was. The man smiled, and raised his coffee mug. "Would you like a cup?"

"Sounds good."

"You sit down." His mother patted his arm and nudged him toward the table. "I'll get it for you."

"What brings you around?"

"Is this about Jillian?" His mom slid a cup of coffee in front of him a knowing smile on her face. "And you?"

"You heard?"

His mom's head bobbed up and down so fast that he almost told her to stop for fear it might fall off. He knew that the town gossip mill was fast, but he didn't think they'd be this fast.

"Iris called last night. Said that she and Alice found you and Jillian on the porch, kissing under the stars." His mom sighed. "So romantic."

Well, this was going to be much easier than he thought. "She's really something special."

"You don't have to tell us." His mom pulled out a chair and sat at the table. "Alice and I couldn't be happier."

"You talked to Ms. Alice?"

"Just got off the phone with her. I'll admit, we're both a little surprised that you've become an item so quickly, but if we've seen anything the last few months with Jillian's siblings, it's that when love is right, it's right."

Blake didn't know what to say. He'd thought this was going to be a hard sell. "I guess so."

"You guess?" His father looked at him over the brim of his mug. "You'd better know. If you ask me, everyone's gone mad. This isn't one of those love at first sight romance novels."

"Well, no, but it's not exactly first sight either. I've known Jillian her whole life."

His father set his mug on the table. "How old was she when you left town?"

"I don't know. Just a kid, but even then there was an intensity to her when she'd watched us play. As if she knew more about life than any of us knuckleheaded boys. I've never forgotten the way she listened to me playing the guitar when I wrote 'Honeysuckle Moon.' I'd swear the awe in her eyes made me believe in myself." Not till this minute did he realize just what her presence that day had meant to him.

His father cocked a brow at him.

"Is it so hard to believe that a man could fall in love with someone like Jillian? She's smart, and caring, and loves her family, and this town. She's amazing." To his surprise, he realized that he meant every word.

"See, dear." His mother elbowed his father as she stood. "Told you he was in love."

In love? Before he could fully wrap his mind around that concept, a sound from the side of the house stopped him cold—first just a rattle quickly followed by a clattering.

"What the heck?" His father turned to the sink window just as his mother pulled the shade.

Another clattering and crash and he knew someone was at the trash cans. As much as he'd like to think it was nothing more than a stray cat searching for scraps, or a neighborhood kid searching for a lost ball, he knew the source was most likely not four-legged or Lilliputian. "Are the blinds open or closed?"

"Closed," his mother responded quickly. "With all the ruckus of reporters yesterday, we never bothered to open them and ignored the knocks at the door."

"They were knocking at your door?" He didn't know why that had surprised him. Padding softly across the house, he peered out between the slats. Holy hell. It wasn't just one reporter, it was a swarm. At least half a dozen of them were camped out on the street in front of his parents' house, their long-lens cameras pointed like sniper rifles. One was at the neighbor's holding a microphone under the owner's nose and another was standing halfway up the drive. No doubt the trash can culprit. This was not the plan. The story was supposed to give them breathing room, not tighten the noose.

He backed away from the window, pulled his phone from his pocket, his only thought—to warn Jillian. Before he could press the button, one of the reporters was knocking at the front door. Oh hell. This was so not supposed to happen.

Jillian stood behind the counter of Heaven Scent, pretending to organize a display of honeysuckle candles that was already perfectly arranged. The shop's familiar, soothing scents did nothing to calm the frantic buzzing under her skin. Through the large plate glass window, Main Street had transformed. What had started as a handful of reporters last night had morphed into a full-blown media encampment, turning her quiet hometown into the set of some bizarre, unwelcome reality show. This was not the plan. The story of a simple visit home sprinkled with a little possible romance was supposed to be a firebreak, a way to give Blake some privacy. Instead, it had become a wildfire, and she was standing at its center.

When Iris and Mildred, bless their gossip-loving hearts, had spread the word yesterday that Blake was just visiting, catching up with old friends, that he deserved some romance after working so hard on tour, it was supposed to give the reporters a simple story and send them packing. Instead, it had the opposite effect.

Now, the whole world, or at least the part of it that subscribed to celebrity news alerts, wanted to know: who was the woman? From her vantage point, Jillian had been watching the interrogations for the better part of an hour. The way she figured it, there were twice as many reporters as yesterday, maybe more. They'd spread out like ants, stopping every single person who walked down the sidewalk. She could hear fragments of their questions through the glass: "Do you know Blake Kirby?" "Have you seen him with anyone?" "Can you tell us about his love life?" "Who's the local woman he's been seen with?"

Jillian watched in a state of suspended disbelief as Mildred McEntire strutted down the sidewalk in full bling, rhinestones sparkling in the morning sun, heading straight for a cluster of reporters near the diner. Jillian couldn't hear what she was saying, but judging by her animated hand gestures and the way the reporters were frantically scribbling notes, Mildred was giving them quite the story.

On the other side of her shop, a ponytail-wearing reporter shoved a microphone in Iris Hathaway's face. Never one to miss a moment in the spotlight, preened and grinning like the Cheshire Cat, she practically snatched the microphone from the startled reporter. "Our Blake has always had a good heart. It's high time he found a nice, down-to-earth girl to settle down with." She was playing her part perfectly, a loyal town elder protecting her own while feeding the machine just enough to keep it purring.

The reporters were relentless. They were stopping everyone. A cameraman nearly tripped over one of the corn hole boards in the park, trying to get a shot of a group of teenagers who were likely making up fantastic stories just for the fun of it. This was getting out of hand. The town was treating it like a festival, but Jillian felt a knot of dread tighten in her stomach. This was insane. Honeysuckle had never seen anything like this. The quiet little town was being invaded by people with cameras and microphones, turning their peaceful Main Street into something that looked like a movie set on steroids.

Her phone buzzed in her pocket, the vibration a welcome distraction. Glancing at the screen, she ducked into the small back office, needing the illusion of privacy.

"It's a war zone out here," she said, her voice low, sinking into her desk chair.

"You're telling me." Blake's voice was tight with a stress that echoed her own. "They're camped out at my parents' house. Knocking on the door, trying to talk to the neighbors over the fence, I think one of them was rummaging through the trash cans. We really stepped in it this time, didn't we?"

Jillian leaned her head against the cool leather, closing her eyes. She could picture it perfectly: his parents, trapped in their own home, their peace shattered by the chaos, chaos she was now a part of. "Iris and Mildred might have overplayed the *deserves some romance* angle a bit. They should have stuck to the original story and said he's hanging around to get to know me better. Now the reporters are on a full-blown mystery woman hunt. They just interviewed Iris Hathaway."

"Oh, Lord, what did she say?"

"That it's high time you found a nice, down-to-earth girl." Despite the complexities of the unexpected situation, a wry smile touched her lips. "I think she was auditioning for the role of your official town spokesperson."

"Great. Just great." He let out a heavy sigh that crackled through the phone. "We have no choice but to stay put. You stay in the shop. The last thing we need is for them to see you and me talking and put two and two together then start camping out at the ranch. We'll never get rid of them."

"Well, we wanted to give them something to chew on." Maybe now would be a good time to hide under a rock for a day or two hundred.

"I was thinking a little appetizer, not the entire menu." She was glad to hear a hint of humor in his voice.

"Eventually they're going to get bored and leave your parents and the rest of the town alone, right?"

"Maybe. Or they'll dig in their heels until they find someone to spill the..." his voice trailed off and it took only a moment longer for Jillian to follow his train of thought.

At the same time, he muttered, "Grams," Jillian voiced, "Sara."

Aw, hell. Could this get any worse?

CHAPTER THIRTEEN

It was impossible to enjoy a decent cup of English breakfast this morning without someone clomping up the porch steps like they owned the place. A cup of lukewarm tea forgotten in her hand, Sara Kirby peered through the sheer lace curtains of her living room window. A gaggle of reporters, looking like a flock of badly dressed, noisy geese, had taken up residence on her lawn, some spilling over into her prize-winning petunias. She'd tried ignoring them, thinking they'd get bored and wander off to bother someone else. No such luck. If anything, they'd gotten louder and more persistent, knocking on her door every few minutes like woodpeckers with poor manners.

They'd been there far too long, shouting questions at her front door and aiming their ridiculous long-lens cameras at her windows. It was an invasion, a complete and utter breach of civility. She had half a mind to turn the sprinklers on, but that might damage their equipment and then she'd have a stupid lawsuit on her hands.

No, this required a different sort of handling. Enough was enough. A few reporters with more enthusiasm than sense weren't going to rattle her.

Setting her teacup down, Sara straightened her shoulders and walked to the hall mirror. Patting her silver hair, ensuring the coif was perfectly in place, she adjusted the single strand of pearls at her neck, and straightened the collar of her crisp cotton blouse. If one was to face a firing squad, one should at least look one's best. She then marched to the hall closet and retrieved what she needed: a sturdy folding chair.

Leaving the chair by the front door, she swept into the

kitchen, poured a tall glass of iced tea, and added a sprig of mint from the pot on her windowsill. Armed and ready, she strode through the living room and unlocked the door. Now or never.

The flock of reporters swarmed the porch steps, a cacophony of overlapping questions erupting at once.

"Mrs. Kirby, is Blake here?"

"Is it true he's got a new girl?"

"Is it serious?"

"Why has he been hiding?"

Sara ignored them all. With a calm deliberation that seemed to momentarily stun them into silence, she unfolded the chair, placed it precisely in the center of her porch, tugged a metal side table beside the chair, set her glass on the table, and sat down. Crossing her ankles, she smoothed her slacks and folded her hands neatly in her lap. After taking a long, slow sip of her iced tea, she leveled a gaze on the most aggressive-looking reporter, a young woman with bright red lipstick and an impatient frown.

"All right," her voice carried easily over the sudden hush, "if you're going to pester me, you might as well do it properly." She scanned the group, her eyes sharp. "Ask your questions one at a time. Enunciate. And for heaven's sake, no interrupting. This is a front porch, not a wrestling match."

The tallest one cleared his throat. "Uh… is it true your grandson is—"

"Five out of ten," she interrupted crisply. "Points deducted for mumbling. Shoulders back, dear, you're not a question mark."

He blinked, straightened his posture, and tried again. "Is it true your grandson is hiding here?"

"That's better. Eight out of ten. My grandson doesn't need to *hide* anywhere. Next."

"Mrs. Kirby, I'm Jessica Wells."

Sara nodded at the woman in bright red lipstick. "Eight out of ten. Good projection, you remembered to introduce yourself, but that lipstick is the wrong shade for your complexion. You'd do better with a pleasant pink. Your question?"

"Can you confirm that your grandson Blake is currently in Honeysuckle?"

"Well, of course, he's here," Sara said with the patience of someone explaining the obvious to a particularly slow child. "Why wouldn't he visit his family when he's not playing music for his fans?"

The cameras clicked frantically. Another reporter, a nervous-looking man with too much hair gel, raised his hand like he was back in elementary school. "Is Blake dating anyone local?"

The man's timid demeanor almost had Sara smiling, he already seemed so nervous, she didn't have the heart to critique him. "My grandson is a handsome, successful young man with excellent manners and a kind heart. Of course the local girls are interested. Have you seen him lately? That boy could charm the birds right out of the trees. Of course he gets that from my side of the family."

"But is there someone specific?" Jessica pressed.

"Well now, that's Blake's business, isn't it?" Sara adjusted her pearls and fixed the reporter with a look that had cowed generations of misbehaving children. "A lady doesn't gossip about matters of the heart. Though I will say this…" She leaned forward conspiratorially, and every microphone strained toward her. "Any girl would be lucky to catch that boy's eye. He's got his grandfather's romantic soul."

The man with the hair gel practically vibrated with excitement. "Can you tell us her name?"

"Can you tell me why you're standing in my flower bed?" she countered sternly with her best sweet Southern smile. "Those are award-winning petunias you're crushing, young man. First prize at the county fair three years running. Their feelings are hurt very easily. Step to the left, if you please."

Looking sheepish, the reproved man shuffled sideways.

"That's better. Now, where are your manners? You haven't even introduced yourselves properly. Didn't your mother teach you anything?"

The reporter, momentarily flustered, recovered quickly.

"Sorry ma'am, Robert Peel—"

A man with a notepad jumped in. "Is your grandson staying here with you? Is he hiding from the press?"

Sara fixed him with a withering look. "Now, what did I say about interrupting?"

For the next twenty minutes, Sara held court like a benevolent dictator, expertly deflecting every question with a mix of Southern charm, subtle scolding, and maddeningly vague non-answers. She critiqued their posture, corrected their grammar, and the reporters, used to dealing with screaming celebrities and slick PR agents, were utterly disarmed.

Though not how she'd expected to spend her day, she couldn't remember a time when she'd had more fun. Blake should sneak around town more often.

"I can't leave." Exasperation hung on every syllable of Blake's words. "These people are crawling around like ants on a picnic blanket."

"I'll go check on Ms. Sara." Jillian glanced at the grandfather clock in the shop's corner. "I'm closer. Besides, with all this commotion, I don't see any customers caring about candles today."

"You don't have to do that," he said with a soft voice.

"I know, but I want to." For a second she thought his silence meant he was not happy with her. She braced for the worst when he slowly enunciated her name.

"Do you have any idea how amazing you are?" His voice was throaty and raw and made her toes curl in her shoes.

"I don't know about that, but I am going to close up. Hold on." Grabbing her purse from her desk drawer, she hurried to the door, turned the open sign to closed, and with a turn of the key in the lock, she was moving down Main Street as fast as she could without drawing attention to herself.

"So far, so good." She felt like a spy in an action flick. Remembering how they skunked Garrett's wife's ex using the phones for communications, she decided that maybe being spies could be a lot of fun. "I'm almost to the corner and no one has shown any interest in me."

"Considering how these reporters seem to be chasing down anyone on the street, I'm going to take it as a good sign that they've not bothered you."

She couldn't agree more. "Almost there," she whispered, her rubber-soled shoes silent on the concrete. At the end of the block, she cornered the building, fully expecting to see the media crowd up the street laying siege to the Kirby house.

The scene that greeted her was so bizarre, so utterly unexpected, that she stopped dead in her tracks, nearly dropping her phone. His grandmother wasn't just handling the reporters; she was conducting them. Sara Kirby sat serenely in a folding chair in the center of her porch, a tall glass of iced tea on a small table beside her, holding court like a queen on her throne. The reporters weren't a swarming mob; they were a semi-orderly, if somewhat bewildered, audience.

"What is it? What do you see?" Blake's voice, tight with anxiety, crackled in her ear.

"I… you're not going to believe this." Jillian bit back the laugh threatening to erupt. "Your grandmother is something else. I'd swear she's holding court on her front porch like the Queen of England. She has a folding chair, iced tea, and she's got every single reporter sitting at attention like they're in Sunday school."

"She what?"

"I'm serious. She's critiquing their posture and correcting their grammar. One guy just apologized for stepping on her flowers." Jillian didn't bother to stifle the laugh that bubbled up. "Blake, she's a lesson in utter magnificence."

Through the phone, she heard him let out a breath that was part relief, and a whole lot of pride. "That's my grandmother. She always was a force of nature."

As Jillian watched, Mrs. Kirby spotted her approaching. A brilliant smile bloomed on her face. Without missing a beat, she raised her voice, a clear, ringing tone that carried easily across the lawn. "I have company now, ladies and gentlemen. And my petunias have had quite enough excitement for one day. Time for all of you to go home and find a real story to cover. Shoo!"

"Jillian," Blake's voice was urgent in her ear, "get inside with her. Fast."

"Already on it." Jillian quickened her pace, waving at Mrs. Kirby like she was an expected guest. "So sorry I'm late."

The older woman beamed. "Right on time, sweetheart. Come on up."

Jillian hurried up the porch steps, acutely aware of the cameras following her movement. Mrs. Kirby stood, folded her chair with practiced efficiency, and ushered Jillian toward the front door.

"Lovely visiting with you all," Mrs. Kirby called over her shoulder to the reporters, quietly closing the door and turning the lock behind them.

"That," Jillian waved a thumb over her shoulder in the general direction of the front yard, "was the most impressive thing I have ever seen."

Sara Kirby simply smiled. "Nonsense, dear. Just a bit of housekeeping." She patted Jillian's arm.

"Hello!" Blake's voice came through the cell phone that Jillian momentarily forgot she was holding.

"Sorry. We're still here."

"And the reporters?"

Jillian glanced through the lace curtains. "Are leaving."

"You're kidding? Maybe I should have Grams march over here and dispatch the reporters still camping out on Mom and Dad's lawn."

"Do you need me, dear? I'm sure I can teach your reporters a thing or two about good manners if you'd like."

Through the speaker phone, Blake chuckled. "Thanks, Grams, but I'm sure it will be fine. As soon as they stop rummaging through the trash, I can probably sneak down the alley the same way I got here. Jillian, since I'm stuck here for the immediate future, you might as well go ahead and update Grams on everything happening."

"Everything?"

"If you don't mind."

She shook her head even though he couldn't see her through the phone. "Got it."

"Thanks. You're pretty awesome yourself."

A few more words and assurances and the call was disconnected. Placing the phone in her purse, Jillian turned to Mrs. Kirby. "About that secret woman the reporters are looking for…"

CHAPTER FOURTEEN

Blake stared out the kitchen window, nursing his second cup of coffee and watching the morning light stretch across the Sweet Ranch. Two days had passed since Jillian's rescue mission to his grandmother's house, and while some of the reporters had apparently gotten bored and moved on to more interesting celebrities, like vultures waiting for roadkill, too many were still lurking around Honeysuckle.

Today was the day. Dr. Crawford's appointment was scheduled later this afternoon in Miller's Creek. Somehow they had to get his grandmother there without creating a media circus that would follow them all the way to the specialist's office.

"Any brilliant ideas brewing in that coffee?" Alice slid a plate of scrambled eggs in front of him and another in front of her daughter.

"Still working on it." Blake picked up his fork, though his appetite had pretty much disappeared along with his peace of mind. "We can't exactly waltz out the front door with Grams and hope nobody notices."

"We could maybe do it in waves?" Jillian shrugged. "I could pick Ms. Sara up and maybe take her to the beauty parlor, get her nails done. Then come back to get you, while Mom goes into town to pick your grandmother up. They'll never think anything of Mom and your grandmother."

"Not a bad idea," her mother nodded, "then we can all meet up somewhere out of town and y'all head to the doctor and I'll head home."

"Something like that." Jillian stabbed at her eggs.

The plan had possibilities. "Better than just waltzing out

the door with her." Though, after his misjudgment on how this talk to the press would go, he was leery to follow any new plan.

Brady, who had been dozing by the back door, suddenly lifted his head. His ears snapped to attention, and a low growl rumbled in his chest.

Coming down the steps, Kade's gaze narrowed at the unsettled dog. "What is it, boy?"

"At least we know it's not you coming home for a surprise visit." Their mother's tone was teasing yet laced with just enough reproof for not having let her know he was coming home. Her gaze turned toward the dog.

Brady rose to his feet, a rigid line from nose to tail. He paced a tight, agitated circle, his gaze fixed on the front windows, the fur along his spine raised. The growl deepened.

Blake set down his coffee cup.

Staring at her son's dog, Alice's spine stiffened.

Jillian shook her head. "Something's not right."

Everyone now on their feet, focusing on the dog, the source of Brady's distress became clear. A figure, silhouetted against the graying dawn, crept across the front lawn, slowly approached the house, and foolishly pressed their nose against the living room windowpane.

"Oh, for heaven's sake," Alice practically growled herself. Wiping her hands on her apron, she marched to the living room. Her expression anything but motherly. It was pure, unadulterated fury.

Blake thought she was going to open the door and let Brady take care of the unwelcome guest. He should have known better. Instead, the woman had gone straight to the gun cabinet, and retrieving a standard shotgun, cocked the loaded weapon.

Years ago, he could have seen Charlie Sweet doing exactly that to protect his family. No sane human being dared mess with the family of a rancher.

By the time Alice crossed the room and flung the front door open, her gun at her shoulder, aimed at the idiot, Kade had done the same, taking his gun with him out the back door, he softly told Blake and Jillian that he would circle around from behind. Another moment and Jillian had her hand gun out of her purse and at her side. The Sweets were ready to defend their hearth and home.

If it weren't his fault the reporters were descending on the family, and he didn't have to go look to know that the fool would be a reporter, he'd almost laugh at the synchronized reactions.

"Excuse me!" Alice's voice carried across the yard with the authority of a drill sergeant. "This is private property. What exactly do you think you're doing with your face pressed against my window?"

The man jumped like he'd grabbed hold of a live wire, tumbling backward. Even from where he stood, Blake could see the guy's face go pale when he spotted Alice with the shotgun.

"I was just—"

"Trespassing," Alice finished for him. "With a camera. On my land. Without permission. I'd take it kindly if you'd take your curious nose and that camera and get off my land before I'm tempted to rearrange it for you."

The man didn't need to be told twice. He scrambled to his feet and ran back toward the road, where the dark shape of a parked sedan was barely visible.

Kade on the corner of the front porch, Jillian now at her mother's side, and Blake thanking heaven that the reporter wasn't as stupid as he looked, they all watched the man leave before turning back inside and calmly returning their weapons to their rightful place.

"Honestly," Alice huffed, "you'd think they'd have better manners." The job done, she turned and headed back to the kitchen as if she'd done nothing more than shoo a stray cat off the porch.

"Well," Blake poured a fresh cup of coffee, then smiled at Alice Sweet, "that's one way to handle the press."

"For now." Jillian chuckled softly. "We may have to rethink how we get your grandmother to the doctor."

The table now surrounded by Sweet family members, sighs and huffs and slurps of hot coffee filled the air, but no good suggestions were heard. Then, a slow grin spread across Kade's face. He looked from Blake, to his siblings, then back again. "They're waiting for Blake Kirby, rock star…"

Everyone slowly nodded, except Carson who rolled his eyes.

A mischievous glint had Kade's eyes sparkling. "Maybe we should just give them what they're looking for."

Kade's mischievous grin was contagious. One by one, the tension around the kitchen table began to dissolve, replaced by the familiar spark of Sweet family ingenuity. An idea, wild and audacious, took shape in a flurry of overlapping suggestions. With a few phone calls to key players, a quiet morning of dread had officially transformed into a mission.

"Okay, so Carson's our primary decoy." Already in strategic mode, Preston looked from his brother to Blake. "You two are the closest in build. They're expecting Blake to leave from here."

Carson, who had initially rolled his eyes, now leaned forward, a slow smile spreading across his face. "What am I wearing for my big debut as a rock star?"

"Something noticeable," Rachel chimed in immediately. "Something they can't miss."

Twenty minutes later, the plan was in motion. From the living room window, Jillian watched as Blake, dressed in khaki pants and a bright pink button-down shirt with rhinestone cuffs, walked out to his rented SUV. At the driver's side door, he slid the dark glasses in place, put his favorite ball cap on his head, and patted his pockets. With a long-suffering sigh visible even from the house, he turned and walked back inside. The bait was set.

A few minutes ticked by. Then it was Carson's turn. Having switched clothes with Blake, he pulled on the dark baseball cap, slid on Blake's sunglasses, and with his head down, strode purposefully to the SUV. He didn't hesitate, just climbed in, started the engine, and pulled away, heading south down the main drive. Jillian held her breath, binoculars pressed to her eyes. Just as Carson reached the main road, two sedans with tinted windows pulled out from their hiding spots and fell in behind him.

"We have a follow!" she called out. A round of triumphant, hushed high-fives went through the room. Phase one was a success.

The real genius of the plan, however, was its scale. It wasn't just about a single decoy; they needed to distract all the paparazzi. While Carson led his tail on a wild goose chase toward the southern county line, Alice activated the town's formidable grapevine.

The first confirmation call came from Iris Hathaway, her voice crackling with conspiratorial glee over the speakerphone. "They're on the move! Young Bobby Prescott just left his house wearing one of those ridiculous hoodies and a pair of sunglasses big enough to land a plane on. One of the reporter vans is right on his tail, heading east!"

"Okay," Alice clapped her hands, "time to head to Sara's. You two duck down in the back seat. I have a good feeling about this."

"Wait." Rachel held up her hand. "Give Jim and me a few minutes head start." Her sister and brother-in-law were dressed to impress. Jim had on the cowboy hat that Blake had worn the last few days as well as dark glasses, boots, jeans, and one of Blake's shirts from the concert tour. Rachel had on Jillian's favorite yellow sundress, a floppy hat and, of course, dark glasses.

Ten minutes after Rachel and Jim were gone, the three of them climbed into the car.

"Here we go." Her mom looked way too happy about all this role playing. Not that Jillian blamed her. The whole thing was just a little bit... tantalizing.

Almost to town, Jillian's phone buzzed. All this excitement was right up her speed demon sister's alley.

"Hey Sis," Rachel's cheery voice came through loud and clear, "we're parked in front of the bakery. I ran in to get some donuts. By the time I came out, there were at least three vehicles following us out of town."

"Perfect." Her cheeks almost hurt from so much smiling.

"And thank Blake for the use of his house." The sound of keys jingling could be heard over the soft music playing. "These poor suckers are so going to think we're you and Blake when we lead them straight to his place near Austin."

"Drive safe." She disconnected the call.

"Y'all missed your calling." Blake shook his head, smiling. "The Barrymores have nothing on you."

Another beep came in. This time it was her mother's phone. "Get that for me, dear."

Jillian dug in her mom's purse and pulled out the phone. Answering, she could hear Iris's voice talking to Mildred. "She must have butt dialed."

"No." Her mom shook her head. "She said she was going to let us listen in."

"Oh, this is rich." Jillian laughed. "Not only are we listening, it's a video call. Her phone is propped up so I can see it all."

"Ooh." Alice whined. "I can't drive and watch."

"She's leaning over the table, practically nose to nose with Mildred. Glancing around before speaking. I can see at least two reporters in the booth behind her."

"Did Alice call you?" Iris asked.

Mildred, who toned down her bling for the event, nodded. "It's all set. They're leaving from the ranch this afternoon. Alice is going to drive them to the airport in Midland."

"Midland?" Blake muttered.

"Shh." Jillian waved him off.

"It's going to be a quick wedding," Mildred continued. "They're flying to Vegas, getting hitched, then flying home."

"Now Vegas?" Blake's brows rose high on his forehead.

"Oh, that Iris is truly brilliant," her mom whispered so only they could hear. "Makes me wonder if she's really with the CIA."

Jillian bit back a laugh as the conversation continued.

"I promised her we'd have the church hall all decked out for the reception."

Mildred nodded, and gleefully rubbed her hands together. "We'll have food, and music, and I'll make my famous chardonnay punch."

"Ooh," Iris squealed. "And white doves and ice sculptures shaped like guitars!"

Biting on her lower lip not to laugh, from the performance these two put on, Jillian almost believed the two ladies.

The reporters in the nearby booth scurried out of their seats and two more people at a table across the way pushed to their feet as well. Another few minutes and the café door slammed shut and Iris and Mildred were almost bent over with laughter.

"Did you catch all that?" Iris asked.

Mildred high-fived her friend. "And that is four more reporters on their way to Midland or Vegas or who knows where."

A broad grin on his face, Blake leaned over and kissed Jillian's forehead. "Miller's Creek, here we come!"

CHAPTER FIFTEEN

"Phase three, ready to go." Still ducked low in the back seat, Blake laughed easily as Alice hopped out of the vehicle and hurried up the porch steps to Sara's house.

A few minutes later, the two women were safely strapped into the front seats, laughing like a pair of school girls.

Never would Blake have thought his grandmother would cooperate with such a crazy scheme. "This is more fun than canasta night," she declared happily.

Alice took the side roads to the edge of town where Kade, already parked waiting for them, leaned against the hood of the old suburban.

Parked beside him, Alice quickly hopped out. "Did you hear?"

Smiling, Kade nodded. "There are more Blake and Jillian impersonators in Honeysuckle than Elvis' in Vegas."

"You got that right." His mother gave him a high-five, then turned to her daughter. "It should be smooth sailing for the three of you from here."

Shifting places, Blake slid behind the driver's wheel, Jillian took shotgun, and his Grams settled comfortably into the back seat.

The absurdity of the last few hours gave way to a sense of cautious optimism. The town had bought them a clear path. Now all they had to do was get to Miller's Creek and back without any more drama.

Plugging the doctor's address into the GPS, Jillian studied the screen, then twisted to glance out the rear window. "So far, so good."

"So, where are we going now?" His grandmother grinned from the backseat.

"Miller's Creek."

Grams' brows dipped into a perfect V.

Hell, she'd been so good, he'd almost forgotten all about the why of this little plot. "Visiting Doc Conroy's friend?"

Heaving a deep sigh, his grandmother rolled her eyes. "Oh, yes. That man worries too much."

Hopeful her momentary lapse was nothing more than the equivalent of him forgetting where he placed his car keys, he refocused on their mission and glanced in the rear-view mirror. The road behind them was empty, stretching back through the dusty Texas landscape. He allowed himself to relax, his hands loosening on the wheel. Maybe, just maybe, their crazy plan had actually worked. Despite feeling more at ease about their escape, Blake continued to check the rear-view mirror every so often.

At first, the road remained empty, but not even halfway to Miller's Creek, he noticed a dark speck in the distance. Most likely it was just another local heading in the same direction, but like your tongue constantly seeking out the gap of a recently lost tooth, he couldn't help but glance in the rear-view mirror more frequently than normal.

After several miles of this, Jillian seemed to have sensed his unease, or maybe she'd just been as concerned as he'd been. "How long has that car been behind us?"

"A while."

Her gaze remained fixed on the side mirror, but she didn't say anything else.

Keeping his speed steady, his eyes flicking between the road ahead and the mirror. The car that had come close enough to determine it was a sedan, maintained its distance, a persistent shadow. It wasn't speeding up, but it wasn't falling back either. A prickle of unease, the same kind he felt when a crowd got too pushy backstage, had slowly been creeping up his spine and settling uncomfortably at the base of his neck.

Out in the middle of stark West Texas, there was no

way to determine if the driver and lone passenger, or at least what he thought was a lone passenger, were just heading to Miller's Creek for some inconsequential reason, or if they were indeed being followed. He didn't like thinking he'd become paranoid, but he liked the idea of being tracked by reporters even less.

Despite not another word said about the sedan, the tension in the car was elevating to the point that Blake could almost hear Jillian grinding her teeth and his grandmother wringing her hands.

Near the edge of Miller's Creek, with more offshoots from the main road leading to the scattering of new residential areas, he hit his blinker. "Time to find out what's really going on."

He made a slow turn onto a narrow, gravel farm road. The bumpy stretch was an illogical route for anyone just passing through.

Jillian's gaze was fixed on the side mirror. "They're turning," she confirmed, the two words dropping like stones in the quiet car.

The knot in his stomach tightened. This wasn't a local. This was a tail. Following the road as it turned and curved, he looped around and came back on a different road to meet the main drag.

"Damn it," he muttered under his breath.

"Still there?" his grandmother asked. There was no need for Jillian to say anything; her gaze had not left the side mirror.

"Hang on." He pressed down on the accelerator. The Suburban bucked and complained, but it picked up speed, dust billowing behind them. This wasn't a panic, not yet. It was a test. He pushed the old vehicle, taking the barren road faster than he should, the frame groaning in protest.

The sedan behind them had no trouble keeping pace. If anything, it gained on them, the sun glinting off its windshield. This was no longer a test. This was a chase.

"Who are they?" Grams asked from the back, her voice remarkably calm, though she was now gripping the back of Jillian's seat.

"Most likely reporters who didn't fall for the decoys," Blake gritted out, his knuckles white on the steering wheel. Determined to shake their shadow, he pressed harder on the gas pedal, watching the needle ease higher and higher on the dashboard.

"There's a sharp curve up ahead." Jillian pointed with her chin, her own hands braced on the dashboard.

Though it had been ages since he'd driven to Miller's Creek, he remembered the curve. A nasty, off-camber turn that came up without warning. He eased off the gas, preparing to navigate it. He glanced in the rear-view mirror one last time. The sedan wasn't following his lead, they were getting too close. Idiots.

The old suburban rocked as he took the turn a little faster than he probably should have. Behind them, the squeal of the sedan's tires could be heard as clearly as if they were riding in his trunk. Coming out of the long turn, about to hit the gas pedal once again, he glanced in the mirror one more time. The sedan clipped the shoulder, the back end fishtailing wildly. For a horrifying second, it tipped up on two wheels, a gravity-defying sculpture of metal and poor judgment, before it slammed back down and flipped, rolling once, twice, and once more before coming to a rest in the dry ditch—upside down.

Blake slammed on the brakes, the old Suburban skidding to a halt on the gravel shoulder, dust swirling around them. The world outside the windshield distorted into a horrifying tableau: the overturned sedan, the plume of black smoke, the sudden, hungry flicker of orange. For a paralyzing second, Jillian's breath seized in her lungs. This couldn't be happening.

"Stay here!" The words were a sharp command from Blake, already a blur of motion as he threw his door open.

Like hell. The thought was a raw, primal instinct. Her hands, clumsy and numb, fumbled with the seatbelt buckle.

"Ms. Sara, call 911!" The words tore from her throat as she shoved her own door open, scrambling toward the back of the Suburban. The ranch truck. Fire extinguisher. Her mind worked in frantic, disjointed bursts. "I'll grab the extinguisher."

He glanced back, his face a grim mask of focus, and gave a curt nod before turning back to the wreck. She wrestled the heavy, red cylinder free from its straps, its weight a solid, terrifying reality in her arms. She ran, her feet pounding against the hard-packed dirt, the acrid smell of burning oil and rubber filling her lungs.

The smoke was thicker now, a choking cloud. She aimed the nozzle at the base of the flames erupting from the car's undercarriage and squeezed, a blast of white powder providing a momentary, blessed relief. Blake was at the driver's side, yanking on the crumpled door, his muscles straining. It wouldn't budge. "It's jammed!" he shouted, his voice strained.

She saw him reach for the door again, then recoil, a sharp curse on his lips. The metal was too hot. A wave of pure, cold terror washed over her. He was going to burn himself. He was going to get hurt. Every instinct screamed at her to drop everything and run to him, to pull him away.

But then, movement on the other side of the wreck caught her eye. Blake ripped his own denim shirt off. The sudden image of his bare torso, muscles taut in the hellish light of the growing fire, was shockingly out of place. He wrapped the thick fabric around his fist and forearm without hesitation. He wasn't just Kade's friend, not just a rock star. He was a man running headfirst into danger.

The fire sputtered back to life, angrier this time. Jillian blasted it again, the extinguisher feeling dangerously light. Help him or get the other one? The choice was a physical tear inside her. She had to trust he could handle himself. She ran to the passenger side, yanking on the hot metal handle, adrenaline giving her a strength she didn't know she possessed. The metal groaned, then gave way with a screech as the door flew open.

Inside, a young woman, a camera still slung around her

neck, was slumped against the dashboard. Jillian reached in, her hands shaking, and fought with the seatbelt buckle. It was stuck. "I can't get it!" she yelled, her voice thin against the growing roar of the fire.

"Jillian, get back!" Blake's voice was raw with panic. Through the smoky haze, she saw he had the driver, a man, halfway out, dragging his dead weight away from the inferno.

"I'm not leaving her!" she screamed at his back, yanking at the jammed buckle. His grandmother was suddenly there, a tire iron in her hand. "Here, child! Pry it!"

Sara Kirby shoved the tool into Jillian's hand. She jammed the flat end into the buckle mechanism, leveraging it with all her might. There was a sharp crack, and the strap snapped free. At the awkward angle, Jillian struggled to get a grip on the unconscious woman. To her surprise, Sara Kirby was at her side, tugging and pulling with a strength Jillian wouldn't have expected for a woman of her years.

They'd barely begun to drag the woman free when the back of the car erupted. It wasn't a Hollywood explosion, but a concussive boom that threw a wave of searing heat and debris at them, knocking them off their feet.

Blake turned and bolted in their direction. "Back away!" His words were barely audible over the angry hisses and pops.

Scrambling to her feet, ignoring the scrapes on her hands and the ringing in her ears, she and Ms. Sara dragged the unconscious woman the last few feet, collapsing a safe distance away. Catching her breath, her gaze darted from the raging inferno to the last place she'd seen Blake. He had to be far enough away to be safe from the blast. He had to be. With him nowhere in sight, panic licked at her racing heart, threatening to steal her last breath, and then, just as suddenly as he'd disappeared, Blake was there, at her side. His hands framed her face, his eyes wild with a terror that mirrored her own. "Are you okay? Are you hurt?" He ran his hands down her arms, checking for injuries, his touch both frantic and incredibly gentle.

"I'm fine," she managed, her voice a hoarse whisper.

"Miss Sara?"

On her feet, remarkably composed, his grandmother slipped her phone into her pocket and dusted at her dress. "I get more scrapes and cuts pruning my rose bushes." Her shaky smile hinted that she might not be as composed as she let on. "I think I'm going to go back to our car and wait for the fire trucks. They should be here shortly." As if summoning help with her words, sirens suddenly blared in the distance.

Waiting a beat to ensure his grandmother was indeed steady enough to return to their vehicle, Blake turned and pulled Jillian against him, his arms wrapping around her in a crushing embrace. She could feel the tremors in his body, or maybe it was her own. He buried his face in her hair, his breath coming in ragged gasps. "Promise me you will never do that again."

Nodding her head into his shoulder, she clung to him, the smell of smoke and sweat and him filling her senses. "Back at you. No more evading paparazzi or fighting with cars on fire. From now on, let the reporters find us."

A slow rumble of laughter rattled against her ear. "*Us*. I like the sound of that."

"Me too," she mumbled into his shoulder.

"Good." He pulled back just enough for his eyes to level with hers. "For what it's worth, Jillian Sweet, I love you."

"Good." She barely had the strength to smile. "Because it just so happens, I love you too."

"Sorry to be a Debbie Downer," his grandmother called from where they'd left the Suburban, "but you may want to settle this later. Like when you have your shirt on. And don't smell like a chimney."

The two chuckled at his grandmother. Truly a formidable woman. Helping each other up, she couldn't bring herself to let go of him. Not now, not ever.

CHAPTER SIXTEEN

The morning air in the Sweet kitchen was thick with the scent of strong coffee and a fragile, unspoken peace. Blake sat at the long wooden table, nursing a mug, the warmth a welcome anchor in the sea of 'what ifs' that had kept him awake most of the night. Across from him, Jillian was quietly stirring sugar into her tea, her movements small and deliberate. Every so often, her gaze would lift and meet his, a furtive, charged look that said everything and nothing at all. He'd come so close to losing her yesterday, just hours after realizing he'd finally found the one woman for him. The thought was a cold knot in his gut that even Alice's coffee couldn't touch.

"Boy, these folks don't waste any time," Carson scrolled through his phone. "The fire, the rescue—it's all over the mainstream news and social media."

Blake's stomach tightened. "How bad is it?"

"Actually, not bad at all. 'Country Star Blake Kirby, his Beloved Grandmother, and Local Woman Risk Lives to Save Reporters in Fiery Crash.' Y'all are being hailed as heroes."

Preston leaned over to read Carson's screen. "There's video footage from someone's phone. Shows you both collapsed by the fiery wreckage. Who the heck took that?"

"By the time the fire was out it could have been any of the firefighters or the line of passersby who had piled up to see what had caused the fireball in the sky." At this point, he honestly didn't care what the news said anymore. He caught Jillian's eye again, and this time neither of them looked away. The memory of her refusing to leave that woman behind, of working together under impossible circumstances, of nearly losing each other to save two strangers—it had changed everything.

"Let me see that." Alice reached for Carson's phone. After a moment, she looked up with tears in her eyes. "I'm so proud of you both."

The quiet moment was shattered by a loud whirring sound that seemed to be getting closer and louder.

"It can't be what I think it is." Kade stood up to look out the window.

The sound grew more annoying, and Brady began barking frantically.

"If you're thinking helicopter," Garrett stood next to his brother, "then not only are you right, it's landing in our front yard."

"Cool!" Rachel jumped up from the table. "Wonder if we can get a ride?"

Jim rolled his eyes and shook his head at his wife. "Down, girl."

The whole family crowded onto the front porch as the helicopter, a sleek black machine, descended with a deafening roar, its rotors kicking up a storm of dust and dry leaves. It settled onto the wide expanse of the front lawn with surprising grace.

"Figures," Blake muttered, the knot in his stomach tightening for a whole new reason. He recognized the logo on the side. "My manager."

"He has a lot of nerve showing up here," Alice said, her voice tight with a protective fury that Blake found deeply touching. "None of this mess would have happened if he'd just respected your privacy in the first place."

The rotors slowed and the side door slid open. Phil Mercer hopped out, ducking his head, a briefcase in one hand and what looked like a ridiculously expensive gift basket in the other. He approached the porch, his usual brisk confidence replaced by a look of strained contrition.

"Blake." The man stopped at the bottom of the steps. "We need to talk." He glanced around at the silent, formidable wall of Sweet siblings. "I, uh... I brought muffins." He awkwardly held up the basket.

Blake crossed his arms, not moving. "You're a little late for breakfast, Phil."

"I know. I'm sorry. For all of it. The 'missing' story, the pressure… it was a bonehead move." Phil's gaze was surprisingly sincere. "I heard what happened yesterday. And about your grandmother. How is she?"

The unexpected question disarmed him slightly. "She's fine. She'll have some tests next week, and then we'll know more." He thought of his conversation with the memory doctor. The physician had reassured Blake that even with a dementia diagnosis, it could be a very slow progression, and with the right care, by recognizing the problem early, they could help his grandmother maintain her quality of life for years to come.

Phil nodded, looking genuinely relieved. "Good. That's good to hear." He took a tentative step closer. "So… the other part of the story the press is running with. Is there really a girl?"

Every eye on the porch swiveled to Jillian. Blake didn't hesitate. He reached for her hand, lacing his fingers through hers and pulling her to his side. She looked up offering a lazy smile meant only for him.

"Most definitely, yes." Blake couldn't hold back his own grin. "There's a girl."

The feel of Blake's hand, warm and sure, laced through hers sent a jolt of pure, uncomplicated happiness straight to Jillian's heart. She leaned into his side, the solid strength of him a comforting anchor in the whirlwind of the last few days. She met his smile with one of her own, a silent, shared acknowledgment that this, whatever this was, was most definitely, very real.

Phil Mercer's gaze moved from their joined hands to her face, a flicker of professional calculation in his eyes. "Well," his manager mode clicked back into place, "that certainly changes things." He turned his full attention to her.

"I hope I'm not speaking out of turn, but I need to talk some sense into this man. We have a situation."

Jillian felt her own smile tighten. "I'm sure you do."

"The European tour is sold out," Phil pressed, his voice taking on an urgent, pleading tone. "Months ago. We're talking stadiums, Jillian. The kind of venues that can set a musician—and his family—up for life. He can't just cancel. And no one," Phil's gaze flickered in Blake's direction, "at least not in his right mind," he turned back to her, "turns down a king."

"The King?" Alice's voice cut in, her eyebrows raised in surprise. "Of England?"

"Of England," Phil confirmed, then barreled on, his focus still on Jillian. "He's a huge fan. It's a massive charity event. The PR is priceless. You can't let him back out of this. He'd be letting down millions of fans, not to mention the band, the crew…"

Jillian felt the weight of it all—the pressure, the fame, the world outside of Honeysuckle that Blake belonged to. A world she was now, inexplicably, a part of. But instead of feeling intimidated, a familiar Sweet stubbornness took root.

"Yeah, well, about that…" she began, an idea, crazy and brilliant, blooming in her mind. She looked from Phil's frantic face to Blake's, who was watching her with a look of amused curiosity. She then glanced at her siblings, their expressions a mix of support and intrigue.

Rachel, ever the quick one, caught on first, a slow, mischievous grin spreading across her face. "You know, Phil, this time of year, Europe can be a great place for a honeymoon."

"Honeymoon?" Phil's face became a perfect mask of confusion.

The word hung in the air, electric. Jillian saw Kade and Garret exchange a look of dawning comprehension. Preston, ever the pragmatist, was already nodding slowly.

"That's right." Blake swung his arm around Jillian. "After the accident yesterday, and with Grams' health in question, we decided," he squeezed her a little more tightly, "that life's too short to wait." Now he straightened his spine and faced all the siblings, especially Jillian's mother. "So, we stopped at the court house on the way home and got a marriage license."

Phil's jaw dropped. He stared at Blake, then at Jillian, then back again, utterly speechless.

"We can't use it for three days," Jillian spoke up. "But after the required waiting period, the plan is to get married right away."

Phil nodded, a hint of a smile on his lips. "Well, I have to say, this changes things. The press is going to eat this up. Rock star marries small-town hero. It's perfect."

"It's not for the press," Blake drilled him with a fierce glare. "It's for us."

Still pressed beside Blake, she shifted slightly and leveled her gaze with his. Hopeful he'd caught on to her idea, she whispered, "What do you think?"

"A honeymoon in England?" he said so softly she was sure only she could hear.

Shrugging, she smiled at him. "It could make everyone happy."

A brighter smile took over his face. "It could. Are you sure?"

She nodded. The plan, so wild and spontaneous, settled over the house with an air of perfect, undeniable logic. It solved everything. Blake wouldn't be letting anyone down, the ranch would get its trust payment, and their sudden marriage would have the most romantic, headline-worthy explanation imaginable. Not to mention, they'd make a king happy too.

"Then it looks like we have some packing to do." Blake looked down at her, his eyes shining with a mixture of awe, amusement, and a love so profound it took her breath away.

"Not so fast." Alice held her hands up. "I have it on good authority that if there's a wedding in this family there will be a party, and if there's a party, there are two women ready to have white doves and ice sculptures."

The whole room—except Phil who had no idea what she was talking about—burst out in deep rolling laughter.

"Fair enough." Blake nodded at his future mother-in-law then looked down at his fiancée, pulled her into his embrace, his mouth only inches from her, he again spoke so softly only she could hear. "As long as you're mine for the rest of our lives, this crazy town can do whatever they want."

"Ditto, Mr. Kirby. Ditto."

EPILOGUE

Strung with what seemed like miles of twinkling fairy lights, the old barn was alive with the sound of laughter and music. Kade leaned against a thick support beam near the edge of the makeshift dance floor, a bottle of cold beer loose in his hand, he merely watched. Home for less than a week, everything still felt just a bit surreal. The peace. The sheer, unadulterated joy that radiated from every corner of the ranch. The complete and utter contrast to the world he normally lived in.

His mom had nailed it when she predicted that Iris Hathaway and Mildred McEntire would be eager to have a hand in the wedding celebration. No surprise to anyone who had heard the conversation in the diner just a few days ago, there were ice sculptures scattered about miraculously not melting in the oven-like temperatures so affectionately referred to as Texas heat. From acoustic guitars, to electric guitars, to twelve-string guitars, the music industry was well represented in ice.

Searching the crowds, Kade easily spotted the bride and groom. He'd known Blake Kirby most of his life. As kids there was no end to the mischief they'd get into. Sneaking out to go fishing when they should have been doing chores, dreaming about futures that seemed impossibly far away. He'd seen Blake perform for crowds of fifty to fifty thousand, and proudly watched his friend accept awards as if Kade had anything to do with Blake's talent and success. He'd also seen his friend with more women than Kade could count. Too many. But the rock star was gone. The kid he'd grown up with was gone, too. In their place was this man who looked at Kade's little sister like she was the only song worth singing. They were in their own world, a perfect, quiet island in the middle of the happy chaos of their wedding reception.

When Blake dipped her low, making her laugh that bright, musical sound that carried over the music, the joy on both their faces was so genuine it almost hurt to watch. This wasn't the business arrangement it had started as. This was the real thing. Never one to believe in love at first sight, with five siblings married and head over boot heels in love, he might be willing to change his mind... maybe... at least for other people.

"They look happy." His mom appeared beside him sipping from a glass of champagne.

"Yeah," Kade spoke softly, "they do."

"You're the only single one left." His mother gave him a sideways glance, complete with teasing grin.

Kade took a long pull from his beer. "I'm not really the marrying type, Mom."

His mother studied him with something akin to X-ray vision that only mothers seemed to have, and that always made him uncomfortable. Finally, breaking the connection, his mother pushed up on her tippy toes, gave him a gentle kiss on the cheek, and turned, ready to walk away. "Don't sell yourself short."

His gaze drifted across the room. Preston, with his arm slung around Sarah Sue's shoulder, whispered something that made her laugh. Behind them, Carson danced with Jess, their son Mason trying to mimic their steps and tumbling into Brady's patient, furry side. Garret and Jackie were by the long food table, stealing bites of cake and grinning at each other like teenagers. Across the way, his sister Rachel was in a heated but smiling debate with Jim, her hands flying as she made a point, his eyes full of nothing but adoration. He couldn't be more surprised by how one thieving, conniving, foreman could have been the catalyst to shifting their entire worlds. Though he would have preferred an easier way to bring about all this love and romance, he wouldn't change the outcome for all the tea in China.

Everything here today was why he did what he did. Fought—literally—to protect this very idea of home, family, and Mom's apple pie. But standing here, an observer on the edge of it all, he felt a profound and unsettling distance. All his siblings were building futures, laying foundations of love and laughter. He was just... on leave. And despite what he'd said to his mother about not being the marrying kind, he was still next. The business of saving the ranch wasn't over. Not yet.

"Looking pretty glum, big brother." Rachel appeared at his side, her husband across the way refreshing their beverages.

"Just enjoying the moment."

"It is a sweet moment, isn't it?" She chuckled quietly. "No pun intended."

A smile reached his lips. They did look sweet together, and it made him damn happy too. Things could have gone south fast with this crazy plan his siblings had concocted.

Preston came to stand beside his brother and sister, his smile even wider than theirs. "Just got some news from the sheriff."

That had Kade and Rachel impatiently waiting on high alert like drug-sniffing dogs on a charter flight from Colombia.

"Well," standing ramrod straight, Rachel glared at her brother, "what did he have to say?"

"They caught two of our wayward hands in Wyoming."

"That's a start." The tension in Rachel's spine eased.

"Oh yes." Preston bobbed his head, his gaze still on the newlyweds dancing. "They were trying to sell that hay baler that disappeared."

"What?" Now Rachel snapped back, her eyes wide, and her hand gripping Preston's arm. "Our hay baler?"

"Who else's?" Preston rolled his eyes at their baby sister. "Dad had a really far reach. The cattlemen's club spread the word. Ranchers all over the country are on alert for our equipment and thank heaven at least one rancher was on the ball. He reeled the hands in, showed interest, asked benign questions, and the authorities in his neck of the woods arrested them both this morning."

"That's fantastic. Two down and three to go." Practically bouncing in place, Rachel slapped her hands together and rubbed them enthusiastically.

Preston turned to face Kade. "Looks like you've cut a break."

"How so?"

"At the moment the baler is evidence, but soon we'll get it back. Since we're doing okay with the baler Jim gave this one for a wedding gift," he flung his thumb over his shoulder in Rachel's direction, "we can get our money back on the recovered baler, or at least most of it, pay off that part of the note, and breathe a little more easily. At least for a while."

All Kade did was slowly nod. He'd have to see the numbers to get a handle on where they stood, but for the moment, he wouldn't lie to himself, it felt good not to have to hunt down a bride just yet.

The song ended and Blake pulled Jillian close, whispering something in her ear that made her stand on her tiptoes to kiss him. The crowd cheered, and when they broke apart, both of them were grinning like teenagers.

Yeah, he was relieved, maybe. Life had definitely taken another sharp and unexpected turn. He simply wasn't sure he—or anyone else—was ready for what was coming next.

MEET CHRIS

USA TODAY Bestselling Author of dozens of contemporary novels, including the award winning Aloha Series, Chris Keniston lives in suburban Dallas with her husband, two human children, and two canine children. Though she loves her puppies equally, she admits being especially attached to her German Shepherd rescue. After all, even dogs deserve a happily ever after.

More on Chris and all her books can be found at
www.chriskeniston.com

Follow Chris' Monday Blog at her website
ChrisKenistonAuthor

Follow Chris on Facebook at
ChrisKenistonAuthor

Never miss a New Release!
Sign up for News from Chris:
www.chriskeniston.com/newsletter.html

Questions? Comments?
I would love to hear from you! You can reach me at:
chris@chriskeniston.com